THE NGAA

And there it was!

A swift-moving sphere of bright blue-white flame burst from the overcast and rose toward him. The color was the same as J had seen the night of Richard Blade's return, but much brighter. The Ngaa —for this must be the Ngaa—seemed to fairly seethe and sizzle with energy.

As the plane leveled out, the Ngaa swung out of sight in the blind spot.

The co-pilot, watching his radar screen, broke in, "The damn radar is going crazy! I can't tell anymore, even approximately, how far away he is or where he's located in relation to us."

"I'd say the Ngaa is getting close," said J. "We may already be within his outer edge."

"Here he is!" Captain Ralston cried.

The wing on his side had become illuminated by flickering blue light and now, as all turned to look, the bright ball of blue-white fire came alongside, not more than a few hundred meters away, drifting with a languid slowness that belied the fact that it was traveling at supersonic speed.

Captain Ralston sighed with relief. "He's going to leave us alone."

The Ngaa slowed.

"Oh, oh," murmured Ralston.

The Ngaa wheeled in a gleaming arc and came rushing toward them, accelerating.

The co-pilot shouted, "He's going to ram us!"

THE BLADE SERIES:

HEROIC FANTASY SERIES

30

An incredible time-space journey to Dimension X!

RICHARD BLADE

DIMENSION OF HORROR
by Jeffrey Lord

PINNACLE BOOKS   LOS ANGELES

BLADE #30: DIMENSION OF HORROR

An original Pinnacle Books edition, published for the first time anywhere.

Produced by Lyle Kenyon Engel

First printing, March 1979

ISBN: 0-523-40208-2

Cover illustration by John Alvin

Printed in the United States of America

PINNACLE BOOKS, INC.
2029 Century Park East
Los Angeles, California 90067

Author's Note

The information given about real people, such
as Jack London, Ambrose Bierce, George Sterling, Clark Ashton Smith and Nora May French,
is factual, taken from their respective biographies.
The reader may draw his own conclusions from
the decidedly odd circumstances of their lives
and deaths, but he may rest assured I did not
make them up.

The rest of the characters are totally fictional,
and I have had my little jokes with the geogra-
phy of London and Berkeley.

DIMENSION OF HORROR

Chapter 1

Ponderously Big Ben tolled midnight. The lean balding man on the couch awoke and sat up in the semidarkness, tossing off his blanket. He swung his bare feet to the carpeted floor and sat a moment in his rumpled undershirt and drawers, stretching and gathering strength, trying to shake off a paralyzing dread that clung to him from a nightmare he only dimly remembered. He had had many such nightmares in recent weeks.

"Damn," he grumbled. "Bloody nuisance."

The only reply was the muffled murmur of the city.

He stood up and groped toward the shadowy mass of his desk. The telephone rang as he knew it would. He picked up the receiver.

"Twenty-four hundred hours, sir," came a bored masculine voice. "You wanted to be called . . ."

"Thank you, Peters. Could you have the car brought 'round?"

"Right away, sir. Main entrance or side?"

"Main. No, wait. Make that the side, on Lothbury."

"As you wish, sir."

He hung up and lit his desk lamp.

His craggy face, illuminated from below, was for a moment a ghastly mask of black and white patterns, a face of unguessable age, the face of a man whose demanding profession had never allowed him the luxury of growing old. Blinking, sighing and shivering in the muggy cold, he peered moodily around his barren office cubicle, leaning against his heavy teakwood desk. There were three chairs: two uncomfortable wooden ones in front of the desk and one comfortable leather-upholstered one behind the desk, his only self-indulgence. No pictures hung on the wall, not even a calendar. The tall black filing cabinets were, as always, locked. The black metal wastebasket was stuffed with paper that

1

would, as usual, be carefully shredded and burned before leaving the building.

The two tall arched windows that ordinarily provided a view of Lothbury's congested traffic now had been transformed by the fog into irregular mirrors that distorted his reflection into a mocking caricature. Looking at this face that was his, yet not his, he felt the dread returning. He wondered, *Is this a hunch? Should I call the whole thing off?* He paid attention to hunches. Because of hunches, he had outlived nearly all the men he had known in his youth, though his was not a profession noted for longevity.

"Not this time," he reassured himself out loud. "My deuced imagination is acting up again. Mustn't let it bowl me over."

He strode to his closet, opened the door, and peered within. There hung his white shirt, his blue-striped Cambridge school tie, his waistcoat, his dark-gray suitcoat, his pinstriped gray and white trousers. His rolled umbrella leaned against the wall, gray suede gloves draped over the handle, next to his dark brown attaché case. All in all, the uniform of a successful stockbroker, if you added the black bowler that rested on the shelf above eye level; but he was not a stockbroker.

A stockbroker would not have had in his closet, hanging casually from a peg, a shoulder holster containing an old Webley service revolver. He kept the weapon cleaned, oiled and loaded at all times, though he had not worn it, except at the practice range, for over twenty years. He did not wear it now.

Instead he shaved, then dressed quickly.

The stockbroker image was almost too perfect. Surely this was one of Britain's captains of industry: vigorous, aggressive, yet imperturbable and urbane! He not only looked his part, he felt it too. Setting his derby on his head at a jaunty angle, he grinned defiance at his reflection. Nothing to worry about. What are a few bad dreams, eh?

As he left his office he locked the door behind him, then, as always, tried it to make sure it was locked.

Outside the Lothbury Street exit a black four-door Rolls Royce awaited him at the curb, polished chrome gleaming. A gray-uniformed chauffeur sprang to attention and, opening the car's rear door, said crisply, "Your car, sir."

"Not so military, Watkins."

"Sorry, sir."

The seeming stockbroker glanced at the building behind

2

him, a towering Victorian monstrosity that had survived two world wars. It had never been damaged or, it would appear, cleaned. On the grimy brick wall a well-burnished plaque identified the New East India Copra and Processing Co. Ltd. There was indeed such a company within, but there was also the headquarters of MI6A, a very special branch of the Special Branch of the SIS, or Secret Intelligence Services.

Once this seeming stockbroker had had a name, but he had all but forgotten it. Now he was known only as "J," head of MI6A, answerable only to the Prime Minister. To even be informed that J existed, it was necessary to demonstrate what the intelligence community called a "need to know," yet J had more than once bent the course of history in Britain's favor, always working quietly, behind the scenes.

J climbed into the Rolls and settled himself into the seat with a grunt of satisfaction.

Watkins slammed the door, then bent over to ask, "Where to, sir?"

"The London Tower, Watkins."

J closed his eyes as the powerful vehicle nosed out into the stream of traffic. He thought, *Everything seems fine, but something's wrong. I can feel it!*

The fog thickened as they neared the Thames, slowing their progress considerably as they threaded their way down Great Tower Street. J made an unsuccessful attempt to read his pocketwatch, then snapped it shut with a muttered curse and jammed it into his waistcoat pocket.

At last the vast angular bulk of the Tower of London complex hove into view, almost invisible in spite of the floodlights that shone on the central "White Tower." That there were eleven other lesser towers clustered around it was something that had to be taken on faith.

At the curb Watkins held the door while J stepped to the sidewalk.

"Shall I wait for you, sir?"

"No. Come back in an hour and a half."

"As you wish, sir."

J watched the red-haloed taillights of the Rolls dwindle and fade, then started toward the rear of the Tower grounds, using his rolled umbrella as a blind man uses a white cane.

Out of the blackness an amused light baritone voice asked, "Nice evening for a stroll along the Thames, eh what?"

"Is that you, Richard?"

"Of course." Richard's familiar heavy platinum cigarette lighter flamed, revealing an ironic half-smile on the younger man's rugged features. This was indeed Richard Blade, calmly lighting a Benson & Hedges, then cutting off the flame with a click.

The men shook hands with a warmth that would have surprised some of J's associates. J had a reputation, for the most part deserved, for being a man without human feelings, able to order other men to their deaths without hesitation. Though he knew it was unprofessional, J had been unable to avoid caring about Blade. Was it because they had worked together so long? J had personally recruited Richard at Oxford, been Richard's superior officer through twenty years of espionage that included some rather sticky capers and more than their share of what the Russians call *mokrye dela*, "wet stuff," executive actions involving bloodshed.

Or was it because J, a lifelong bachelor, had made of Richard a kind of unofficial adopted son? J had pondered the question often but had never discussed it with anyone: a gentleman does not express his feelings.

The two men walked slowly in silence.

At last J said, "I understand it won't take very long."

Blade laughed.

"And what," J demanded, "do you find so amusing?"

" 'Won't take very long.' Those are, if memory serves, the exact words you used to summon me by phone for the first one of these little experiments. 'A few hours at the most,' you told me. Those few hours have become years, sir."

"That's true. I'd forgotten. Your memory never ceases to amaze me." *And not only your memory,* J reflected. According to the doctors' reports from Blade's last physical, Blade continued to be the most nearly perfect physical and mental specimen in MI6. A lesser man would not have survived the incredible punishment Blade had suffered in mission after mission. A lesser man would long ago have demanded a transfer to less hazardous duty.

J added, "You're free to refuse the assignment."

Again the mildly amused voice. "I know that. I'm always free to refuse, but I never have."

J thought, *How many times have I sent you out into God knows where? Twenty-five? Thirty? I've stopped counting. Someday you'll pass through that bloody machine and you won't come back.*

J's eyes were becoming accustomed to the darkness . . . or

4

had the fog lifted a little? He could make out the outlines of Richard Blade's massive six-foot-one-inch frame, clad, it appeared, in the usual light wool Burberry coat with no hat. As Blade inhaled, the tip of his cigarette glowed brightly, faintly illuminating his clean-shaven, square-cut features. Blade was smiling, but it was an odd little smile, a smile that reminded J of the ancient Roman gladiator's motto, "We who are about to die salute you."

Two other overcoated men materialized out of the fog. A flashlight snapped on, blazing in J's eyes. An emotionless voice said, "Good evening, sir. Identification please."

While the Special Services men examined his papers, J shifted impatiently from one foot to the other, angry at the cold, angry at the dampness, angry at the delay. Blade, by contrast, appeared abnormally calm and impassive. Feverishly J glanced around, seeking something in the real world that would justify the uneasiness that had followed him out of the world of sleep.

The Special Services men returned the documents. "Everything seems to be in order, sir. May I trouble you for this week's password?"

"Raven," answered Richard Blade, pocketing his own documents matter-of-factly.

"Countersign nevermore," said the man.

"Very good," said Blade.

"Follow me, please."

The man gestured with his flashlight beam.

The Special Services men led and J and Richard Blade followed. They trudged along an ancient causeway, past a grassy sward that had been, before it was filled in, a moat. They passed through a grove of leafless skeletal trees interspersed with hulking cannons from some bygone era. On their left arose the outer walls of the Tower complex, the top lost in whiteness overhead. On their right, beyond a stout retaining wall, flowed the River Thames.

A ship was out there, heard but not seen, its diesel engines rumbling softly as it went by. A moment later the waves from its wake broke against the shore with a rhythmic hiss.

This was not, J reflected, a site he would have selected for England's most secret project, had he been given the choice. In the afternoons, when the tide was out, that narrow sandy shore became a beach on which antlike hordes of children from Stepney and most of the East End swarmed, laughing and shouting and wading and feeding the ill-tempered swans.

5

Above the beach, in the narrow strip of park between river and wall, tourists from every country in the world strolled and gossiped and took pictures. God, how they took pictures! Once J had seen two Russian sailors taking snapshots of each other in the very shadow of the entrance to the secret project.

"One moment, sir," said the taller of the two agents. They halted before a heavy grillwork gate beneath the broad archway at the base of Saint Thomas's Tower. The gate was secured by a chain and combination padlock at the center, and the taller Special Services man now busied himself with the tumblers while his partner held the flashlight. Richard leaned forward to watch; J knew Blade could memorize the combination of a lock by watching someone open it just once, and that he practiced this skill whenever the opportunity presented itself.

Richard said softly, "The Tower of London frowned dreadful over Jerusalem."

"What's that supposed to mean?" J demanded.

"It's poetry," Blade explained. "William Blake wrote those lines way back in the eighteenth century. He rather caught the spirit of this place, don't you think?" Richard had memorized an astonishing amount of classic verse at Oxford, and had a habit of quoting it at the most unlikely times. "Blood! Horror! Doom! That's what we think of when we hear about the Tower of London, and small wonder. Some of the grandest rascals in English history passed through this old Watergate on their way to torture, imprisonment or beheading. That's why it's called the Traitor's Gate."

J thought, *The Traitor's Gate! How apt. Two Russian spies have passed through here in very recent history and penetrated to the heart of the secret project, in spite of all our fanatic security precautions.* Neither had returned alive to reveal what went on there, but next time . . .

J shuddered.

"There you are, sir," the tall man said. The gate opened with a creak. J and Richard Blade stepped inside.

The Special Services men locked them in and vanished into the fog, returning to their posts. In the yellow light from a bare electric bulb in the ceiling, Blade and J proceeded onward, locating the almost invisible secret door that led into a long, dim, damp tunnel, into a maze of sub basements, and finally to the familiar door of the elevator.

J pressed the elevator button, aware that the button was photographing his thumbprint as he did so. Far below a

6

computer would compare his print with that of everyone who had a security clearance for the project and, deciding that J was "all right," would, in a few seconds, send up the elevator.

The elevator arrived with a rush.

The door slid open. J and Blade entered. The elevator dropped through two hundred feet of solid bedrock with a speed J had never quite gotten used to, then slowed to a stop. They stood in silence until the heavy bronze door hissed open.

They stepped out into a brilliantly lighted foyer, bare except for a desk and two chairs freshly painted an uninspiring olive drab.

"Where's Lord Leighton?" Blade wondered aloud.

"I fancy he's waiting for us in the computer area," said J.

Blade moved through the foyer with a catlike lightness that belied his powerful two-hundred-and-ten-pound mass of rock-hard muscle and bone.

They walked briskly through long corridors, passing closed doors, closed doors and more closed doors. J could hear muffled voices behind the doors, the clatter of typewriters, the whir of spinning computer tapes, but within the hallways not a soul was to be seen. No human guards were needed. Electronic sensors followed their every step, checking and rechecking that they were who they were supposed to be, and were going where they were supposed to go. As long as the sensors functioned, no stranger could enter these passages without setting off an alarm, no matter how careful he was.

At the end of the final passage, a massive door slid open automatically for them and they entered the central computer area. J glanced around and frowned.

In these rooms surrounding the heart of the whole project J was accustomed to seeing a crew of technicians hard at work, but now there was nobody here. In fact the computers themselves had changed. They had been changing slowly over a period of time, but this was the first time J had really noticed.

The consoles, which had once been so large they filled the rooms, had shrunk and become fearfully silent, though the lights that blinked and glowed and the screens that displayed everchanging patterns, numbers and words seemed to indicate that everything was turned on and running. J understood. Bit by bit diodes and transistors had replaced big bulky tubes, and had been in turn replaced by tiny integrated circuit chips that contained whole libraries of preprogramming in an area the size of a thumbnail. Everything had become smaller, cooler, quieter, yet at the same time more powerful. Now the last step had been taken. Automation had replaced human control, and the last human operator had been banished.

"Lord Leighton?" J called out. The bare rock walls threw back a disquieting echo.

"There he is." Richard pointed.

Lord Leighton, in a rumpled green smock, had blended in so well with his beloved computers he had been almost invisible. The machines were not, as they had been, dull gray with crackled finishes, but, except where a spot of gleaming chrome or spotless red plastic showed its contrast, all were in the same muted matt green as Leighton's smock.

"Ah, welcome, welcome!" Lord Leighton came scuttling forward. "How do you like my new toys?"

Leighton was a monster, a troll, a grotesque Quasimodo lurching along with a halting, crablike gait on legs that had never quite recovered from a near-fatal childhood attack of polio. Yet under his high balding forehead with its sparse strands of white silky hair pulsed a brain of terrifying power. In the field of computer technology Leighton might well be the greatest genius England—indeed the world—had ever seen. Every device in this project had begun as a gleam in these dark-pupiled yellow-rimmed bloodshot eyes that now stared up at J through the thick distorting lenses of a pair of steel-framed glasses.

J replied uncertainly, "Very pretty toys. Very pretty."

Leighton extended a small dry claw and J shook hands with him. Toys? Was it proper for a man of Leighton's advanced age to go on prattling about toys?

Now Leighton was shaking hands with Blade, bubbling over with gargoyle enthusiasm. "I've solved it at last," the little man boasted. "At least I think I have!"

"Solved what?" Blade was grinning, caught up in the scientist's excitement.

"Our most challenging problem of all. Before this we've never been able to send you to the same place twice, except by accident. If I'm right in my theories and calculations, I can now, once I've established the coordinates, send you again and again to the same destination. The replicator is ready!"

J raised a questioning eyebrow. "Really?" J had all but given up on this part of the project. From the beginning the replicator had been top priority, yet it had never come to fruition.

8

J did not become infected with Leighton's high spirits. Instead he looked around once again at all the new equipment, and his sense of impending disaster returned stronger than ever. New equipment? That meant untested equipment, hazardous experiments made more hazardous. Again and again Lord Leighton's demonic device had hurled Richard into other universes, other dimensions that no one before had dreamed existed. Somehow it had dragged him back each time, sometimes seconds before some particularly unpleasant death. The very names of the places he'd been rang with a shimmering occult sonority. Tharn! Sarma! Jedd! Patmos! Royth! Zunga!

Where were these places? In the distant past or the distant future? On planets that circle other suns in this galaxy or some other? In divergent or parallel time tracks, worlds that might have been? In universes that coexisted with this one, but which we could not see? J had no idea. With each trip the whole bloody business had become harder to understand. Even Lord Leighton, full of glib explanations at first, had gradually become as baffled as Blade and J.

Yes, though nobody honestly knew what they were doing, the experiments went on. Perhaps the time had come to halt, to stop doing and start thinking.

But Leighton was clutching J by the arm, saying, "Come along, old chap. The best is yet to come." J allowed himself to be half-dragged toward the innermost computer room, the place where the impossible had happened already so many, many times.

J hung back when they reached the massive entrance door. "Perhaps it would be better to wait, to be careful . . ."

It was Blade, surprisingly enough, who answered, "No! I *want* to go."

J studied the younger man a moment. It's said one can become addicted to anything. Was Blade addicted to the machine? Here was a possibility they'd never considered, a dangerous possibility. And what if Blade found on the "other side" a world he liked better than stodgy old England? Could the computer bring Blade home against his will?

The door opened.

Blade and Lord Leighton went in, J trailing behind.

Lord Leighton had been chattering on all this time, and Blade, listening intently, had been nodding at intervals and asking questions in a low voice.

"As you see, the most drastic changes are the ones I've

9

made in here," said the hunchback proudly, gesturing toward the place where once the familiar electric-chairlike device had stood. With alarm J noted that a new contraption occupied the center of the room, a sort of upright Iron Maiden or Egyptian mummy case, but with a tangle of wires attached to it.

Lord Leighton was explaining, "This case is molded so that it fits you exactly, Richard my boy. No one else can use it. And all the electrodes that I used to attach to you, one at a time, are now pressed into positive contact with your body automatically when the box closes."

"Interesting," said Blade. "A definite improvement."

"A part of an overall plan," said Leighton. "The replicator, you see, is not a separate unit to be plugged into a pre-existing whole. It is a strategy for the organization of the entire process. When I put the electrodes on by hand, there's no way I can ever put them on exactly the same way twice. I, myself, was inadvertently introducing variation into something that must be exactly the same every time. And look here." He gestured toward a completely remodeled control console. "I have eliminated the red sliding switch you've so often seen me throw an instant before you—er—departed."

"Then how do you start the final sequence?" asked Blade.

"I don't. Once the program is fed into the computer memory banks, only two switches remain active: Program Start and Program Stop. And when Program Start is pushed, the preliminary sequences begin and run themselves out, one after the other. That's nothing new. The innovation is that the impulse that starts the final sequence comes directly from the computer, automatically, when it comes to the end of the prelims. I never touch the controls unless I think something is going wrong. Then I hit Program Stop. Normally everything is completely automatic, including the closing of the box. The computer even turns itself off after you've been launched."

Blade asked, "What's the point of that? Oh wait, I see. The machine repeats every step exactly the same way every time, and thus should produce the same result, so long as nobody changes the program."

Leighton beamed up at him. "Exactly! You should have been a scientist, my boy. You have the mind for it. What we had failed to see was that no human being could do things as perfectly as a machine, not even a human being as unusual as myself."

Blade smiled at Lord Leighton's unconscious egotism.

The scientist continued, "The only variation that remains is your thoughts. You must try to think of the same things every time you're going to the same place. Do you think you can do that?"

"I can try."

"Excellent! Tonight we'll only do a quick one. We'll send you through for ten minutes, no more. Then the computer will bring you back. Do you think that in ten minutes you can somehow make note of where you are well enough to recognize it again?"

Richard nodded. "There's always a moment of wild dreamlike disorientation before my mind focuses on the other world, but I don't think that takes up much objective time. There used to be an undetermined period of unconsciousness after I passed through, but I think that's dwindled down to nothing or next to nothing. I believe I made the trip to the Empire of Blood without blacking out at all, and the customary headache passed away very quickly. As Dostoevsky once said, 'Man is the only animal who can get used to anything.' Is that all you want me to do? Look around and see where I am?"

"That's all."

"Then ten minutes should be quite enough."

"Good. We'll bring you back and, when you're ready, we'll send you through again with exactly the same program. Unless I'm sadly mistaken, you should go to the same place both times, and if you do . . . "

Blade finished, " . . . all our work will not have been in vain. We'll have ourselves a means of transportation, not an unusually expensive form of Russian roulette."

"Exactly. Any questions?"

Richard shook his head. "No. Compared to my previous missions, this one looks like a piece of cake."

"Then I'll activate the preliminary sequences." Leighton's forefinger moved toward the Program Start button. "Richard, if you'll strip down . . . "

J burst out. "Confound it, you two! Can't you listen to me for a moment?"

They turned to look at him with mild surprise. "What's wrong, J?" Richard asked, puzzled.

J understood that puzzlement. Blade was not used to seeing his superior upset. Normally J maintained a facade of British reserve and imperturbability that made him seem hardly

11

human. "I don't know what's wrong, but something is. I feel it!"

Leighton said coldly, "Feelings have no place in a laboratory."

Blade laid a hand on J's arm, saying softly, "I know there's danger, sir. There's always danger. But when you're pushing into the unknown, you have to obey the unwritten law of science."

"Which unwritten law?" asked J.

"The law that says, 'If you *can* do it, you *must* do it,'" said Blade. He turned away from J and headed for the changing room. This time J made no attempt to stop him. Richard had missed the sarcasm behind J's remark. Leighton pressed the button. A green-glowing digital clock lit up and began the countdown.

Stiffly J asked Lord Leighton, "What generation computer is this now?" J did not really want to know. "Tenth? Eleventh?"

"A new series," said Leighton.

"Really?"

"I call it the KALI Mark I."

"Kali? Why do you call it that?"

"That's what the initials of its scientific name spell out. Kinematic Analog Leighton Integrator."

"Kali is the name of a Hindu goddess."

"You don't say! What sort of goddess?"

"A goddess of destruction!" said J grimly.

"Coincidence, old boy. Pure coincidence. Doesn't mean a thing."

Richard Blade emerged from the changing room, naked. In times past he'd worn a loin cloth into the machine, but the cloth had always remained after he'd departed. Even the coat of black grease smeared all over his body to prevent electrical burns was no longer needed.

With a glance at the rapidly changing countdown clock, Leighton said sharply, "Quick, Richard. In you go. We don't want to have to abort the mission, do we?"

Richard stepped into the upright case and stood in the gleaming copper-colored many-segmented interior, saying, "Like this?"

Leighton's finger hovered over the Program Stop button, but he said cheerily, "That's it. Now lean back slightly. Perfect!"

The three men waited.

12

The clock flickered. It was into the low numbers now. Ten. Nine. Eight. Seven. On the count of six, without warning, the heavy curved door of the case swung shut with a thump. Five. Four. J became aware of a low hum. Three. Two. One. Zero.

There was no sound to mark Richard's departure, but J was almost blinded by that mysterious golden blaze of light he'd seen so many times before, a light that seemed not to come from the case, but from everywhere and nowhere, as if a giant rip had opened in the very fabric of space, letting some unknown sun shine for an instant into the underground room.

The case swung open, and J saw, with eyes that had not yet adjusted back to the normal intensity of light, that Richard Blade was gone.

He turned to Lord Leighton and commanded, "Start the sequence to bring him back."

"No, no. I can do nothing. KALI will bring him back. It's all in the programming," said Leighton. J noticed that Leighton's mottled face was pale. "Sit down. Try to be comfortable. This goddess, as you call her, is on our side. She can count out ten minutes far more precisely than either you or me."

In a daze J pulled out the folding spectator seat, installed for his benefit on one wall, and sat down. The digital clock, he noted, was counting down again.

J and Lord Leighton carried on a trivial, absent-minded conversation punctuated by long silences during which J often pulled his pocketwatch from his waistcoat pocket and compared it with the digital clock on the instrument panel, as if the upstart electronic timepiece might require correction from an older, more reliable source.

As the flickering green numbers began counting the final thirty seconds, even this conversation ceased. Both men turned an expectant gaze toward the open case.

Nine. Eight. Seven. Six.

The case closed.

Five. Four.

The humming had begun.

Three. Two. One. Zero.

Again the searing golden light filled the room, fading almost instantly, but an odd bright blue-white haze remained, unlike anything J had seen before. The haze, glowing and pulsating, appeared to be seeping rapidly out from the seams where the cover joined the case, and there were tiny glittering points of light in the haze, like dust motes in sunbeams. The haze could have been steam except for its color, yet it did not move like steam. It moved purposefully, independently of any current of air in the room.

J sprang to his feet, alarmed.

The case was opening.

The cloud of haze, with a speed J would not have believed possible, streamed out of the case and off toward the exit with a curious high rushing sound, like an indrawn breath but much louder. As it passed, J felt a curious tingling sensation, like static electricity on an exceptionally dry day. Glancing at the back of his hand, he saw the hairs rise like a nest of charmed serpents and sway as if they had lives of their own.

Half-turning toward Lord Leighton, J blurted, "What . . . . what was that?"

The little scientist did not answer. His attention was entirely on the case, which now stood fully open. In it stood Richard Blade, but a Richard Blade inexplicably changed. Though he had been gone only ten minutes his angular chin was shadowed with at least a day's growth of stubble.

Blade had often returned from the X dimensions dazed, unconscious or even dying, but never before quite like this. His eyes were open, but fixed and staring, and his expression was one of abject terror, every feature contorted into a mask of fear, the flesh pale and gleaming with sweat, the muscles in his neck standing out like cables.

J took a step forward. "Richard?"

This could not be! Richard had always been the one man in all humanity who could not be frightened by anything.

"Richard?" J called again.

Blade did not reply, but went on staring blindly at nothing.

Lord Leighton advanced carefully, right hand clutching an air pistol, loaded, as J knew, with tranquilizer darts. It had been standard equipment in the laboratory for some time now. "Easy does it," Leighton said gently. "Everything's all right, Richard. You're home."

At last Richard moved, leaning out of the case like a huge falling tree, landing on his hands and knees with a force that must have been painful.

Lord Leighton took aim.

"Wait," J said, raising a restraining hand. "I don't think he's dangerous."

Richard's head lifted, tangled black hair dangling over his glistening forehead.

14

"What's wrong?" J asked gently. "You can tell us, Richard."

Leighton had not lowered the pistol. "He's a big man, J. If he gets rough . . . "

"He won't get rough."

Richard raised a tightly clenched fist.

"Get back, J," Leighton warned.

The fist came down, striking the floor with an alarming thud. When the fist raised Richard's knuckles were bleeding.

Then Richard began to scream, frightful howls, more animal than human, that echoed and reechoed in the hard-walled cavern room. Again his fist crashed down, and again and again, each time leaving a red stain on the floor. At last he half-turned, as if about to attack the delicate structure of the device from which he had emerged.

Leighton squeezed the trigger.

Chapter 2

The tranquilizer took a surprisingly long time to take effect, though the dose was literally enough to stop a horse. The dart pistol had originally been brought into the project when Blade had returned from one of the X dimensions with a horse. This animal, perhaps the largest thing ever brought back from the "other side," had nearly wrecked the laboratory before the tranquilizer gun had arrived, and Leighton had reasoned that Blade might someday return with another horse, or something worse, and had kept the pistol, never dreaming that he would have to use it on Richard.

When Richard's fit of violence finally subsided and he lay in a crumpled, semiconscious heap, Leighton made a hasty inspection of KALI's components in the immediate area, but found no damage. J looked on, stunned.

Leighton pressed the button on the intercom and summoned a squad of technicians with a stretcher and a straight jacket. Blade's powerful body, such an asset in the field, had become a liability, even a danger.

Still unable to speak, J followed as Blade was carried to the elevator and transported to the hospital complex an additional hundred feet below the computer rooms. Lord Leighton hobbled at J's side, keeping up with difficulty on his stunted legs, but J was only dimly aware of him.

As the elevator door hissed open at the bottom of the shaft, they were confronted by a red-faced fat little man in tennis shoes, white slacks and an appallingly flowery short-sleeved Hawaiian shirt. This was Dr. Leonard Ferguson, Principle Psychiatric Officer for Project Dimension X.

The doctor raised an eyebrow. "A straight jacket? We're not following our standard operating procedure, are we?"

"Obviously not," Leighton snapped.

J shared Leighton's dislike of Ferguson. Neither could he forget that Ferguson had once attempted to force Blade's

16

retirement from the project on the grounds of an "impairment of decision-making powers." In a certain Report 97, Ferguson, with the support of his team of consulting psychiatrists, had predicted that Richard's mental condition would "in the future lead to some dysfunctional withdrawal at a crucial moment."

J had overruled Ferguson, but now . . .

J glanced at the fallen giant on the stretcher and thought with anguish, *Perhaps Ferguson was right!*

J's gaze swung to the fat man's face in time to detect the faintest trace of a triumphant smile.

"This way," Ferguson said crisply, starting down the hall. "His bed is ready."

J slept and woke again, there on the couch in the Staff Lounge. In the underground hospital there was no night, only an endless artificial day. When he awoke the second time, J took out his pocketwatch and inspected it with bleary incomprehension for a considerable period before realizing that it had stopped.

He dragged himself to a sitting position and looked around. The room was empty at the moment, but he harbored dim memories of doctors and nurses coming and going, conversing in low voices so as not to disturb him.

He groped in his pockets for a cigar or one of his well-loved pipes, then realized he had left every form of tobacco back at his office in Copra House. He muttered a curse, remembering his own words. "I understand it won't take very long."

With a sniff of mock self-pity, he stood up and brushed himself off, then slipped on his gray suitcoat, which he had carefully hung over the back of a chair to avoid wrinkling it. After tying his Cambridge tie as neatly as he could without a mirror and generally straightening himself up, he went in search of someone who could tell him what was happening.

After prowling up one door-lined passageway and down another, he finally came in sight of Dr. Ferguson, who was coming out of one of the rooms, deep in worried conversation with a burly white-clad orderly.

"Dr. Ferguson!" J called out, breaking into a trot.

The fat little man looked up and smiled without warmth, at the same time dismissing the orderly with a gesture. "Ah, there you are, old man. Before you say another word, I've

17

been instructed to tell you to call Copra House. Your secretary is rather worried about you, I think, though I told her you were . . . "

"Copra House can wait, Ferguson. How is Blade?"

Ferguson's smile wilted slightly. "Come along to the Lounge, there's a good chap." He took J gently by the elbow. "We really must have a chat, you and I."

J shook off the pudgy fingers, but did come along as Ferguson guided him back to the Staff Lounge, seating him on the same couch where he had recently been sleeping.

"Coffee?" the psychiatrist asked.

"No thanks. Just answer my question."

"I think I'll have a cup. It's been a long day." He turned the spigot on the large white percolator and stared with distaste at the unsavory black brew that splashed into his cup.

J growled, "I've had about as much as I can take of your patronizing bedside manner, doctor."

With a sigh Ferguson crossed the room and drew up a chrome and plastic chair in front of the couch, then sat down and sipped his coffee, regarding J with troubled eyes. At last he said, "This was bound to happen, sooner or later."

"What was bound to happen, damn you!" J leaned forward.

"The subject does not respond to any of the usual treatments. I've tried to proceed with the customary debriefing under hypnosis, but your Mr. Blade cannot or will not cooperate. As nearly as I can determine, he is suffering from a case of complete amnesia."

"Amnesia? You mean he can't remember what happened to him in the X dimension?"

"If that was all, we'd have nothing to worry about. We've evolved routines to deal with that. No, this is a different kind of problem, a different order of magnitude, you might say."

"You mean he can't remember his name?"

"His name? Why, my dear boy, he can't remember the English language! He can't remember not to wet the bed!"

"But you have drugs. You have Leighton's bloody memory machines."

Ferguson sipped and grimaced. "Yes. Quite. We tried them of course. I even had a go at shock therapy."

"Shock therapy? You used shock therapy on Blade?"

"Yes. I gave him a bit of a buzz. Thought it might help, but it didn't." He shrugged fatalistically.

"But there must be something . . ."

"I'm open to suggestions. My own little bag of tricks is

18

empty. True amnesia is rare, you know, except on the telly and in films. There actually is no treatment of choice for it. Thanks to all the experiments you and Leighton have been doing on this poor chap, this hospital probably knows more about such things than anyone else, but it seems that, as much as we know, it is not enough."

"Damn you, Ferguson!"

"Damn me? You're projecting, old man, as we say in therapy. If you must damn someone, damn yourself. This is all your doing, you know."

"What are you saying? Blade is my friend. If there's a living soul I care about, it's him."

"Really? You've a funny way of showing affection, if you'll pardon my saying so. Downright kinky, to use a layman's expression. But that's how it goes in Her Majesty's Service, doesn't it? England is everything, the individual nothing. If you're angry though, I don't blame you. A useless emotion, anger, but it hits us all now and then. I've a lovely little pill here." He reached for the breast pocket of his flowery shirt. "It'll grow rose-colored glasses on the inside of your eyes."

J edged away. "No, thanks. I'll be all right."

The psychiatrist took out a plastic bottle filled with white oval capsules. "You know, J, I use these little rascals myself. Perfectly safe, one at a time. And someday, if jolly old England gets a bit much for me, I can swallow a dozen at a gulp and kiss the whole bloody mess goodbye." His tone had been growing steadily more bitter, but now his mood changed abruptly and he smiled again, stuffing the bottle back in his shirt pocket. "But if I tell you my troubles, you'll probably send me a bill for listening. I would, if I were in your place. It's your friend Richard Blade we should be talking about."

"I'm glad you finally realized that," J said acidly.

"I'm not giving up on the poor chap. I'm sure we'll think of something if we sit around and scratch our heads a while. Hmm. Seems to me I recall hearing about a similar case. Wasn't there another one of your men who came back from the X dimensions with much the same symptoms before I started working here?"

J nodded, remembering. "That's right. We were training a fellow named Dexter as a replacement for Blade, but the first time he went through Leighton's bloody machine, he came back screaming 'The worm has a thousand heads! The worm has a thousand heads!' The man was definitively bonkers, and remains so to this day. We've got him tucked away in a sanitarium in Scotland."

"I'd like to examine your Mr. Dexter, after I've studied his file." The fat man leaned back reflectively. "Dexter and Blade may follow a common pattern."

J said sharply, "Are you telling me that Blade is going to spend the rest of his life tucked away in some sanitarium?"

"Not necessarily. I have a better chance than the team that worked on Dexter. I have more data. The state of the art in my field has progressed somewhat. No cause for undue pessimism, but on the other hand we shouldn't expect any overnight casting out of unclean spirits. By the by, who was on the team that handled Dexter?"

"Team?" J laughed mirthlessly. "There was no team. In those days the only psychiatrist in England with a security clearance high enough to work with us was a Dr. Saxton Colby. Colby handled the whole matter personally, without consultation with anyone."

Ferguson shook his head, frowning. "Bad show. No help for it now, though. Could I speak to Dr. Colby?"

"I don't know."

"You don't know? Why on earth not?"

J shifted uneasily. "We don't know where Colby is. We put him in charge of a testing program for candidates for training for the project, potential replacements for Blade. To make a long unpleasant story short, Colby did not develop any viable replacements, but he did develop a few—ah, personal vices—which required his being taken off the project. Nothing nasty, so far as I can recall, but we sent him back to private practice, carefully wrapped in the Official Secrets Act. As to his present whereabouts I haven't the foggiest notion."

Ferguson burst out laughing, much to J's annoyance. "Do you mean to tell me that after all your paranoid security screening, you ended up with a lunatic for your one and only expert on sanity? Oh that's delightful!"

J said coldly, "Our screening can examine a man's past, but not his future. We don't use crystal balls, you know."

"You should! You should!" The little psychiatrist sobered with effort. "And, though for some reason I've never been able to fathom, your MI6A is called an 'intelligence service,' you've unleashed this mad scientist upon an unsuspecting world and now you don't even know where he is. Really, old boy, the mind boggles!"

"If you want to talk to Colby, we'll find him, Doctor Ferguson!"

"Do that! It could be there is a reason why a man sane enough to pass all your tests should suddenly develop these odd vices immediately after treating this Dexter fellow. We have an expression in our profession: 'Loony germs rub off.' What were these vices anyway, if I may ask?"

"If you must know, he was cultivating a taste for nude orgies."

"My word."

"We heard stories. I sent a man down to check, and there was old Colby, capering in the moonlight out in the woods, naked as the proverbial jaybird, along with a number of like-minded associates of both sexes. Well, you know how it is in the service. A little eccentricity is regarded as charming, but anything kinky opens you up to blackmail. The KGB does more than scripture can to keep us on the straight and narrow path, if you see what I mean. We had to let him go."

"Of course. But tell me, exactly how many associates of both sexes were there?"

"I don't recall. Around a dozen. What difference does it make?"

"Probably none, but if there were twelve of them, six male and six female, that would make up a witches' coven. Witches are rather fond of—as you put it—capering in the moonlight in the woods, buns in the breeze. I'm told the Old Religion is still very much alive in Scotland."

J glanced at Ferguson suspiciously, thinking, *He must be joking.* Ferguson, however, was not smiling. J muttered, "I dare say. Scotland never has been truly English."

The psychiatrist waved this remark aside, continuing, "I have another question. This Dexter fellow, was he . . ."

J interrupted, "I've a question myself, Doctor Ferguson. Can I see Blade?"

"Certainly."

"When?"

"Right now, if you wish. In fact, I'd like to see if he shows any sign of recognizing you. If he does, the prognosis could be much more favorable than it is at present." He heaved himself to his feet. "Follow me."

As they entered the corridor, the public address system pinged and began announcing, "Dr. Ferguson wanted in Room Twenty-four. Ferguson to Twenty-four." J noticed an odd note in the voice, a note of subdued panic.

21

Ferguson frowned and hastened his pace, saying in a puzzled tone, "That's Blade's room."

As they neared Room 24, a burly white-clad orderly emerged from inside, caught sight of Ferguson and J, and broke into a run toward them calling, "Dr. Ferguson! Come quick!" The man was alarmingly pale.

"Calm down, damnit," Ferguson snapped. "Get a grip on yourself." He slapped the frightened orderly on the back somewhat more roughly than the occasion demanded, then proceeded to the door of Room 24, J close behind him.

A cluster of orderlies and nurses huddled together in the doorway, murmuring in worried voices. Ferguson and J pushed through the crowd into the small, brightly lit room. J noted with relief that Richard Blade was apparently unharmed, strapped down in a bed, staring vacantly into space.

Ferguson was demanding angrily, "What is all this nonsense, anyway?"

Three of the nurses began speaking at once, trying to explain, a moment before J's gaze fell on the cause of their near-hysteria.

"My God," J whispered.

A large massive white steel dresser lay overturned on its face to the left of the foot of Richard's bed. Above it, near the ceiling, J saw a deep gash in the plaster wall from which pulverized plaster was sifting down in a rapidly diminishing cascade.

One of the nurses, a disheveled redhead, stepped forward as the others fell silent. "I heard a crash in here, sir," she said. "I was in another room down the hall, but I came running. When I entered the dresser was . . . it was . . ."

"Go on, woman," J prompted. "It's all right."

"The dresser was *floating slowly through the air,* settling gently to the floor where you see it now," she finished.

"Was there anyone in the room?" J demanded.

"No, sir. Mr. Blade was here of course, but he was strapped down to his bed. There was nobody in the hall either until a moment later, when every staff person on this ward showed up."

"She screamed, sir," the burly orderly explained.

"I suppose I did," the nurse admitted apologetically, looking down.

Doctor Ferguson was examining the dresser. He shook his head slowly and let out a low whistle. "This is a heavy piece of furniture. We had to move it when we repainted the room a few months back. As I recall it took four strong men to lift it." He turned his gaze to the gash in the wall. The powdered plaster was no longer falling. "Yet it would appear that someone picked the thing up and threw it across the room, smashing it against the wall up there. I can't believe it." He faced the nurse. "Did you say you saw it floating slowly through the air?"

"She didn't see nothing like that, did you, luv?" The orderly slipped a protective arm around her waist.

"Yes, I did!" she insisted.

"She's excited, that's all," the orderly said. "She ain't crazy. When she calms down . . ."

"We do have one other witness," Ferguson said thoughtfully. "Your friend Blade, J old boy. Blade saw it all. If there's anyone can confirm or deny her story, it's him."

J stepped forward. "Richard? Can you hear me? If you can, give me some sign."

Blade did not reply, but did appear to be aware that J was speaking to him. At least, his eyes focused on J's face.

J tried again. "You must have seen what happened here just now. Tell me, Richard. Tell me."

Blade's blank eyes remained on J's face, but his features were expressionless.

"Tell me," J repeated.

J stared into Richard's eyes for a long time, waiting for an answer, or at least for some flicker of recognition.

At last, with an angry shrug, J turned away and strode from the room.

In the lounge he found a wall phone, and after securing an outside line, phoned his secretary at Copra House.

"Could you send the Rolls over to the Tower to pick me up?"

"Right away, sir." Her voice was cold, businesslike.

"Then call our man at Heathrow Airport and have him make ready the Lear jet. Tell him to file a flight plan for Inverness."

As he hung up, J silently admitted that he should be sending an agent on this mission, rather than going himself. *But,* he mused, half-smiling, *everything's so nebulous. I need to get a feel for it personally, first-hand, if I've any hope of understanding it.*

He went to the elevator, pressed the button, and waited,

listening to the rush as it came down. Abruptly, though he had heard no one approach, he thought he saw, from the corner of his eye, someone standing at his right.

He turned to speak, but there was nobody there.

The elevator door slid open. Glancing uneasily around, he stepped inside. As the elevator ascended with a sickening acceleration, he thought bleakly, *Are the loony germs rubbing off on me? I could have sworn someone was there!*

At fourteen hundred hours, in a light rain, the Lear jet touched down at Inverness Airport. Opening his umbrella, J disembarked and hurried for the hangar, leaving the pilot to tie down and make arrangements. The sanitarium had sent a car—a Rover—and a chauffeur, a big fellow with a pot belly and no hair. J guessed he was an old MI6 man in semi-retirement; former SIS men often had a wary look about the eyes and a body that had once been trained like an athlete's, but had been let go to seed, and this sanitarium functioned largely as a place where used-up agents were put out to pasture.

As they drove inland, cruising swiftly along the glistening wet macadam roadway, J leaned forward and spoke to the back of the man's head.

"Have you been working for the sanitarium long?"

"Long enough, sir."

"Do you like the job?"

"I've no opinion about it, sir."

"No opinion?"

"No, sir. I mind my own business . . ." Left unspoken but strongly implied was: *Why don't you mind yours?*

J settled back smiling, confident he was with his own kind.

The rain continued. The countryside became wilder and more mountainous and the farms fewer and farther between. Leaving the main highway, the Rover wound its way upward over roads that were no longer in good repair, that lapsed at times into little more than mud and bare bedrock. There was no sign of human habitation now, except for the road itself, not even the herds of black-faced sheep J had glimpsed earlier, let alone the dour bearded shepherds with their barking collies.

Gray day shaded into night with no perceptible break before the lighted windows of the sanitarium finally hove into view. The Rover bounced and jounced through the wide front gateway and braked to a stop. Through the rain J could with difficulty make out the looming bulk of an ancient

24

manor, irregular in outline and half-timbered in the Tudor style.

Again J was forced to sprint for shelter, the big chauffeur puffing along protectively by his elbow. A thick oak door swung wide to admit him, then closed behind him with a hefty thump that echoed disturbingly in the high-ceilinged vestibule. As the chauffeur went out again into the storm, a white-suited orderly obligingly closed J's umbrella and helped him out of his wet raincoat.

A tall white-haired man in a dark tweed suit came forward, hand extended in greeting. "Ah, so you're the one they call J, the chap everyone whispers about but no one is allowed to speak of. I'm delighted to see you're an ordinary human being after all."

They shook hands vigorously. J said, "Yes, my ordinariness is England's most closely guarded secret."

"My name is Dr. Hugh MacMurdo. I'm in charge here, as you no doubt know. You probably know more about me than I do myself!" He had a trace of a Scotch accent peeping out from behind his carefully correct BBC standard English. "Copra House phoned to tell me to expect you. I've had supper kept warm for you. You must be starved!"

"I could do with a bite," J agreed, sniffing the air. "Is that mutton I smell?"

"Indeed it is, old boy. If you've no taste for mutton you've a hungry time ahead of you here. We eat like regular crofters. Turnips. Oatcakes. Barley scones. And we've a most amazing pudding the Highlanders call Sowans."

Chattering of trivia, he ushered his guest down a long dim corridor and into a spacious dining hall where a fire blazed cheerily in a huge stone fireplace. Additional lighting was supplied by candles in heavy bronze candleholders at intervals along a stout lengthy central table. Gesturing toward the candles and fire, MacMurdo explained, "We make a virtue of necessity, so far as lighting goes. The electricity here is none too reliable, particularly during a storm." He seated himself at the head of the table. "There's just you and I here. The rest of the staff dined hours ago, but I gather that's all to the good. Copra House gave me the impression you have some rather confidential questions to ask me."

J sat down at his right. "Quite so, doctor."

"If some rascal claims we are mistreating the patients, I deny it categorically."

"Nothing like that. It's Dr. Saxton Colby I'm interested in."
J picked up knife and fork.

"Ah, my scandalous predecessor!"

"Yes. Were you working here when he was in charge?"

"I was his administrative assistant. In military terms, I suppose you'd call me his second-in-command."

"Then you knew him well."

MacMurdo chuckled. "I had no part in his off-duty peccadillos, if that's what you mean." He began eating.

"Still, you might be able to tell me if he was involved in any way with witchcraft."

MacMurdo looked up sharply, then sat back with a sigh, chewing his food with the air of a wistful cow. At last he said softly, "So you guessed it, eh? You're a clever bunch up at Copra House. I should have known you'd keep rutting about until you came up with the whole truth. But how did you know?"

"One of my associates, a certain Dr. Ferguson, noticed something odd."

"Ferguson. Of course. A good mind, though one cannot call him a gentleman. Those shirts . . ." MacMurdo shuddered. "You see, we all know each other in the psychiatric fraternity. You've heard the term 'global village'?"

"Please, doctor," J said gently. "Don't try to change the subject."

MacMurdo ran nervous fingers through his disheveled white hair. "Was old Colby involved in witchcraft? Up to his neck, I should say." He took a hasty swallow of his dinner wine, as if to bolster his courage.

"But when we were investigating him, you said nothing about it."

"No, I didn't. No one on the staff did. We get rather clannish up here all by ourselves, cut off from the outside world. We protect each other as much as we can. It seemed to us Colby might eventually live down a reputation as a swinging single, but a warlock is another matter. It's not an image that inspires confidence."

"So you all covered up for him?"

The doctor nodded slowly. "We did. And it was worth it, I think, though now I suppose you'll can the lot of us."

"No, your jobs are safe enough. Loyalty means something to me, too. Team spirit and all that. But I must know all you can tell me about Colby and this witchcraft business. It's become beastly important all of a sudden. To begin with, how did Colby manage to conceal his interest in the subject when we were investigating him for his security clearance?"

"Well, that investigation took place before he got into it. You found nothing because there was nothing to find. It was here at the sanitarium he first started mucking about in the Black Arts. One week he was as straight a man as you or I. The next week he was studying to be a second Merlin. The human mind is my business, old boy, and I can't begin to explain such a complete transformation."

"So it happened suddenly, eh? When was that?"

"I can't recall the date without consulting my files, but it was right about the time you sent us that poor soul Mr. Dexter."

"Dexter?" J said sharply.

"I see you remember him. I'm not surprised. He was a prize, that one. Most of the time he sat around looking at the wall, but now and again, without warning, he'd explode into a screaming fit, kicking down doors and howling about some worm that had a thousand heads. He was a big strong lad, at least when he first got here, and it took four or five of us to subdue him. Once he damn near strangled one of our orderlies to death."

"What was Dr. Colby's diagnosis?"

"Diagnosis? You know the old saying, 'When in doubt, diagnose schizophrenia.' In that sense, your Mr. Dexter was a schizo of the paranoid persuasion, but between us, sir, that was no more than a label we stuck on the case to cover up our own total bafflement. One thing we were sure of. Dexter was afraid. He was literally insane with fear. What was he afraid of? I haven't a clue."

"And what was the treatment?"

"Treatment? Why, we protected ourselves from him as best we could. That was the treatment. After the first day or two, Mr. Dexter was kept doped to the gills, and after a couple of weeks we eased off on the sedation bit by bit to see what would happen, finally cutting him off altogether. He was a regular sweetie after that. Sat on the edge of the bed staring at the wall and said, when he said anything at all, that same damn phrase about the worm with the thousand heads. In short, the man was little better than a vegetable. Colby felt somewhat guilty about how we handled Dexter. Said it would have been better not to dope him up so. sometimes you can reach a man that's angry, but once he switches off the world, you can set fire to his clothes and he won't notice. But you've got to understand this Dexter was a giant, a regular King Kong. He was afraid of something. Who knows what? But we were afraid of *him!*"

J mused thoughtfully, "Dexter was a very special man, Dr. MacMurdo. There's only one other like him in the world."

MacMurdo lowered his voice. "Dexter was being trained for something, wasn't he? And there was an accident, wasn't there? Colby never told me anything, but I guessed that much. It was so long ago. Surely you can tell me now."

J shook his head. "No, I can't. It's still classified information, and besides, if I told you I'm afraid you'd lock me in here and never let me out." He laughed raggedly.

MacMurdo recommenced eating, obviously annoyed. "Keep your little secrets," he muttered, speaking with his mouth full. "See if I care. Anyway, Dexter had nothing to do with Colby taking up witchcraft. There were plenty of other things happening around here about that time. Dexter was the least of our worries."

"What do you mean?"

"As you probably know, no old house in Scotland is complete without one or more ghosts. This sanitarium is no exception. MI6 has owned the manor since World War II, but the family ghosts don't seem to realize that. They lie low for years, then suddenly they stage a grand comeback, howling and swinging chains and throwing the furniture around just like old times. If you ask me, that's what set Colby off. The ghosts. For about two weeks this place was a madhouse in more ways than one. Crashing. Banging. Funny lights. Voices muttering things in foreign languages out of thin air. Strange faces in the mirrors. Even a fire that started, so they say, by spontaneous combustion! It burned up four rooms in the east wing before we could put it out. Could have brought the whole place blazing down around our ears! I can't say who was seeing more things that weren't there, the inmates or the staff. I saw a few things myself. I swear I did."

"I don't doubt it," J said, thinking of the heavy dresser that had crashed against the wall in Blade's room. "And Colby's interest in witchcraft began during this period of haunting?"

"After the haunting," the psychiatrist corrected.

"After? I don't understand."

There was a long uncomfortable pause, then MacMurdo reluctantly began, "First I have to tell you Colby had once had a daughter, back before his divorce, when he was finishing his schooling at the University of California in Berkeley."

"A daughter?" J prompted, puzzled.

MacMurdo nodded gravely. "Jane was her name. She was about ten years old when she died, there in her bedroom looking out over the San Francisco Bay. Colby used to tell me about her again and again, about the view the poor child had had of the Golden Gate Bridge and all. Jane took an overdose of sleeping pills and died by that window. Nobody could say whether it was suicide or an accident. She didn't leave a note."

J broke in, "But what's that got to do with . . ."

"The witchcraft business? Well, along with all those traditional Scottish spooks and ghosties and things that go bump in the night . . . along with all of them came Jane Colby. Dr. Colby saw her. He talked to her. He went for long walks with her in the hills."

"You mean he said he did all that."

"No! He did it! I swear. I saw the lass myself." His Scottish accent became more pronounced when he was excited.

"Are you sure?"

"I never saw her close up, but once, in broad daylight, I saw Dr. Colby on a far-off hillside, walking hand in hand with somebody or something, and when he came back to the manor, he told me who it was. I had to believe him. Wouldn't a man know his own daughter?"

"Are you saying you saw a ghost in the daytime?"

"These weren't ordinary ghosts. Daytime or nighttime, it was all the same to them. That's why, for two weeks, we hardly slept for two hours out of the twenty-four. There was always something happening. Toward the end, though, the haunting tapered off."

"Why was that?"

"How should I know? All I can do is pass on to you what little Jane Colby told her father."

J leaned forward expectantly. "Yes? Yes?"

"She said she could only come through from the other side for a short time. She said she was cut off from her roots, and that a flower cut off from its roots must die."

"By Jove!" J thumped his fist on the table. "So even a ghost has limitations!"

"Wait. There's more. She said it was up to Colby to open up the gate and keep it open. Then she'd return to him and stay with him forever."

"And he turned to witchcraft, thinking that witchcraft

29

could open the gate to the other world!" J was triumphant. At last the whole unthinkable mess was beginning to form some sort of pattern, incomplete yet with an otherworldly logic of its own.

"You've guessed it," MacMurdo admitted ruefully. "Witch-craft was very much alive in those days around here. It still is, as a matter of fact. Last month, while I was in town for supplies, I saw a witch on the telly being interviewed by a reporter, as if she was a bloody film star! But poor Dr. Colby was losing faith in them before your man came nosing about here and caught him with his pants off at a ruddy Witches' Sabbath. They'd promised him a lot, but hadn't given him anything but a bad head cold."

"So that's the story?" J stroked his chin thoughtfully.

"That's the story. I know Copra House retired him into private practice after that, but I have no idea where he went. Do you?"

"No, but from what you've told me I can make a good guess."

"Wherever it is, I'm sure he has continued his quest for a gateway to the other world. He was a strongly motivated man, sir. A very strongly motivated man."

J agreed. "Yes. Guilt plus love equals compulsion."

"Well said!" MacMurdo pushed back his chair and stood up. "If you've no more questions, I must say good night. I have to be up early tomorrow, as usual. We're somewhat understaffed."

"I understand."

"The night man in the hall will show you to your room." The psychiatrist turned to leave.

"Wait." J raised his hand. "I do have one more question. I doubt if it will do any good, but could you let me see Dexter tomorrow morning?"

MacMurdo halted in the doorway, surprised. "Of course not."

"Why not?"

"I thought you knew. Dexter is dead."

It was J's turn to be surprised. "You don't say! When did he die?"

"Last Friday. After years of sitting around like a stuffed animal, he suddenly started screaming again and smashing things. Caught the night staff completely off guard. Before they could do anything either for him or to him, the poor chap died of convulsions. We did an autopsy, but except for the fact that he was dead, your Mr. Dexter appeared to be in excellent health. Now if you'll excuse me . . ."

"Did you say Friday, doctor? What time Friday?"

"As I recall, the time of death was exactly one-forty A.M. Friday morning. I can check the records."

"Never mind. I'm sure you have it right."

"Good night then, and as pleasant dreams as could be expected under the circumstances."

"Good night, Dr. MacMurdo."

Dexter had died within minutes after Blade's return from Dimension X.

J stared numbly at his half-empty plate. The only sound was the steady drumming of the rain on the windowpane.

Chapter 3

London that morning was gray under the diffuse light from the featureless overcast sky. The pavements were wet and hissed as the motorcars and lorries passed. Colors were muted; even the normally bright red of the double-decker buses. A cold unfriendly wind sent skirts whipping and hats flying.

J stood at the second floor window of Lord Leighton's ancestral home at 39½ Prince's Gate, Kensington, puffing morosely on one of his beloved pipes—in defiance of his doctor's orders—and staring down at the leafless trees in Prince's Gate Crescent. From where he stood he could see hardly anything that had not been there when he was young, yet he knew Kensington had changed. Little by little its quiet residential streets had been invaded by a ragtag army of tradesmen; their antique markets and garish mod "boutiques" were everywhere, particularly along the once-respectable High Street and Kensington Church Street.

The antiques, in J's opinion, were mostly trash, but it was the human trash attracted by the boutiques that depressed him. Boys who dressed like girls, girls who looked like boys, shadowy vague androgynous young people who cowered in doorways, sucking on marijuana cigarettes like babies sucking pacifiers. They'd been called different things at different times. Teddy Boys. Mods and Rockers. Even, borrowing a term from the Yanks, Hippies. Their names changed, yes, but always there were more of them, and with numbers they grew steadily bolder until now armed children in packs hunted through the streets day and night, hunted women, hunted the old, the handicapped, the helpless. The crimes of Jack the Ripper had horrified Victorian England; now they would probably pass unnoticed, too commonplace even for journals like *The Sun*.

On Tower Hill, across from the Tower of London, J had sometimes paused of late to listen to ranting apocalyptic evangelists call London a new Gomorrah, and in certain moods he'd slowly nodded agreement, thinking, *Yes, we're ripe for destruction, the whole bloody gang of us.*

At such times Armageddon had seemed, if not inevitable, at least dreadfully desirable. The only question remaining to be debated was, "What form will the avenging angels of destruction take?"

Standing at the window, J thought, *Will they be the ghosts of little girls who killed themselves? Or will they be invisible giants who throw the furniture around?*

Behind him, in the dim interior of the old house, Lord Leighton was on the phone to Number Ten Downing Street.

"No more experiments? But sir, don't be a damned idiot!" The hunchback's voice was outraged, irascible.

In spite of his depression, J smiled. Few indeed were men with the gall to call the Prime Minister of England a damned idiot as openly as that. Lord Leighton had never been the sort to vent his spleen in anonymous letters to the *Times*, and the older he got the less he seemed to care about etiquette and "The Proper Forms."

Leighton managed somehow to calm himself, though his mottled face turned dull red with the effort. "Yes, sir. I understand perfectly. It is you who hold the purse strings." He paused, then, "Be good enough to save your platitudinous political slogans for the electorate, sir. It is they who hold *your* purse strings." Another pause. "As always, your merest whim is my most imperious command, sir." The sarcasm was harsh and unconcealed. "And good day to you, too, sir."

Leighton hung up, banging down the receiver.

J, who had turned away from the window, said mildly, "I gather the PM is unhappy."

Leighton flung himself into a tall-backed Chippendale chair. "We should never have told him what happened to Blade."

"He would have found out sooner or later, and he would have been even more miffed if we'd kept it from him."

Leighton glared up through his heavy glasses. "Things were different when Harry was PM."

J sighed. "Quite." The man they called Harry had held the reins of power when the project had begun, and had been behind it wholeheartedly, laying out the seed money with a marvelously open hand. His successors had been harder to please, each one more "economy-minded" than the last, particularly since the project, after years of work, seemed no nearer than at the beginning to reaching any firm conclusions about the nature of the X dimensions.

Leighton regarded his own blurred reflection in the polished surface of his desk, grimacing with distaste. "We don't look very attractive to these young chaps that try to fill the Prime Minister's shoes these days. Tell me, J, are they getting younger or are we getting older?"

"A bit of both, I expect."

A brooding silence fell, during which the only sounds were the distant rumble and beep of the traffic and the faint pop and crackle of the low-burning coals in the grate. Leighton's gaze turned moodily toward the tall narrow window that looked out on Prince's Gate Crescent.

Finally Leighton said quietly, "He gave us an ultimatum."

J answered lightly, "Either we shape up or he trims our budget. I know that story by heart by now."

"This time he's not talking about trimming. This time he's talking about shutting up shop altogether."

"Good Lord," J whispered.

"Yes, he's talking about putting an end to Project Dimension X, once and for all. If we can't bring Richard Blade back to normal within two weeks, he'll lock us out of the Tower of London complex and throw away the key."

J felt a curious numbness. A thousand times he'd hoped, he'd almost prayed—and he was not a praying man—that something would happen to terminate the project that put Richard, the nearest thing to a friend J had ever had, repeatedly into danger. Now it seemed J would get his wish. Why wasn't he happy? He shuffled over to the grate, picked up a poker and began aimlessly rooting around in the fire. He muttered tonelessly, "All that time, energy and money wasted. All Richard's risks gone for nothing." He looked up suddenly. "But we still have two weeks, you say. We can bring in one of those boys we've been training and send him through the machine. Maybe he'll make it through. Whatever happened to Richard, it happened over there, in that other world. That's where the secret lies, so . . ."

Leighton raised a restraining hand. "The PM thought of that. He has forbidden us to send anyone else through."

"The devil you say! How in the bloody blazes are we supposed to cure Richard if we can't find out what happened to him? The answer is there, on the other side, and we have to be able to go looking for it!"

"So you think the PM is a fool?"

"Worse than a fool! I can't find a word . . ."

"It may surprise you, but I can see his logic. That's the curse of imagination! One can see the opponent's logic every time. Damn near paralyzes a man! Here's how he reasons. Blade is the only chap who ever went through into the X dimensions and returned alive and sane. Now Blade is out of the picture. Ergo we have no one we can safely send through, and moreover if we have no one we can safely send through, we actually have no project. We're all done and we might as well go home."

"Did you tell the PM about the flying dresser? About what happened to poor Dexter?" J demanded.

"Heavens no! If he believed me he'd shut us down as a public menace this very day. If he didn't believe me, he'd send me up to Scotland to act as Dexter's replacement in the giggle factory. Thank God I managed to keep my mouth shut about that part of it at least." He laughed nervously. "I haven't even told you everything that's been happening."

J carefully replaced the poker in its stand and straightened up. "Then tell me, Leighton, damn you."

"Better sit down first, old chap," the scientist advised dryly, tobacco-stained teeth showing in an unpleasant grin.

J took a chair and waited expectantly.

Not looking at him, Leighton said awkwardly, "The fact is that since you've been gone, a lot has happened in the underground lab and in our little hospital. To begin with, Blade shows no improvement whatsoever. Dr. Ferguson has been doing as much as anyone could, which is almost nothing, and all he can tell us about the cause of Blade's amnesia is that it's caused by fear. Blade saw something on the other side so awful his conscious mind cannot accept it, something that's trapped in his subconscious and trying to get out. You could say Blade can't remember it with one part of his mind, but can't forget it with another."

J was annoyed. "That's nothing new, is it? I'm no psychiatrist, but I could have told you all that."

"There's more. From the moment of Blade's return until now the project has been harassed by a veritable plague of poltergeist phenomena."

"Poltergeist?"

"It's a German word for "playful ghost," and indeed it would appear that a full battalion of playful ghosts has been running amuck in the installation. We've had more furniture tossed around. The VIP lounge is a ruin! Unexplained mark-

35

ings have appeared on the walls, looking for all the world like the scratches of gigantic claws. Mysterious fires have been starting all over the hospital complex. One started right before the eyes of one of the nurses, and scared her half to death. Another started in a chemical storeroom. Thank God the fire alarm sounded before there was an explosion. We put that one out not a moment too soon. We've been hearing odd noises, too. Thumpings. Bumpings. Whooshings. And at all hours of the day and night. I myself have heard what sounded like someone whispering to me in a foreign language, but when I looked around there was nobody there. The oddest thing of all was when one of the nurses met a little girl in one of the passageways. They exchanged greetings and it was a moment before the nurse stopped to ask herself how a little girl could get into such a closely guarded place, deep underground. The nurse searched high and low, but the little girl was nowhere to be found."

J mused, "Too bad we don't have a photograph of Dr. Saxton Colby's daughter."

Lord Leighton squinted. "How's that? Oh, I see what you mean. Do you think those two little girls might be one and the same?"

"I'd be surprised if they weren't, the way our luck has been running."

Leighton continued, "I've fed all the data on the poltergeists into the computer, and they've detected a pattern."

"A pattern? What sort of a pattern?"

"There seems to be a kind of sphere of energy in the complex Everything that requires a great deal of force, such as the moving of heavy furniture, happens near the center of the sphere. A little further out we find lower-energy phenomena, such as fires and scratches and odd noises. Everything that happens at the outer edge of the sphere could be accounted for as strictly mental; voices, the little girl and so on."

"The little girl was strictly mental?"

"She could have been. Remember, nobody actually touched her. She could have been an illusion. The computer also detected a definite trend in all these happenings."

"What kind of a trend?"

"The sphere is growing, slowly but steadily. In fact, this morning, quite early, we began to hear the whispering for the first time in the computer section. The computers, as you know, are a good hundred feet closer to the surface than the hospital. This thing, whatever it is, is gradually working its

36

way upward. Unless it changes its rate of growth, it should start to manifest its presence in the streets of London some time late the day after tomorrow, at least in the neighborhood of the Tower. What we do then I have no idea."

"At least we have some data to work with."

"You like data? There's one thing more, and I don't think you'll care for it. At the exact center of the sphere—the exact center, mind you—is our friend Richard Blade." He added softly, "I think we should face the possibility that Blade is the source of the trouble."

"And what then?"

"To protect London, we may have to kill him."

J put down his pipe, which had gone out unnoticed. It toppled over in the ashtray on the desk, spilling cold ashes. J had anticipated the direction Leighton's logic would take, but now that the conclusion had been reached, he felt sick with horror. His voice shaking, he said hoarsely, "I cannot accept that."

"Better one man than hundreds."

"The thing has killed no one yet, Leighton. It has damaged property, but it has killed no one. Before we take a human life, we must be certain human life is in danger, particularly . . ." He hesitated.

"Particularly if the life is Blade's," Leighton finished. "The thought of a poltergeist frisking about in the computer rooms like a bull in a china shop cannot help but appall me, but of course you're right." These words were uttered in such a faint gloomy voice they were almost inaudible. J realized with a chill that it had been his beloved computers Leighton had been worried about all along, not the people of London.

J stood up and began pacing the floor, head lowered and hands clutched together behind his back. "If Richard were sane, all this nonsense might stop. Let's suppose it's a kind of demonic possession."

"Demonic possession!" Leighton snorted with contempt. "There's no such thing as a demon!"

"Need I remind you, sir, that something came through KALI with Blade. Didn't you see it? A kind of blue glowing cloud?"

Leighton nodded reluctantly. "I saw it."

"That cloud may be our enemy. Perhaps it somehow draws its energy from Richard, and that's why it clings so close to him. If Richard came to his senses, the thing might no longer be able to maintain its hold on him. At worst we'd have

Richard's help against it, and he's been to the thing's home territory. He may know its weaknesses, if it has any."

"Dr. Ferguson has tried every treatment known to psychiatry. Nothing seems to help."

J halted before the hunchback and frowned down at him. "But has he tried the resources of simple humanity, my dear Leighton?"

"What resources?"

At the moment he had asked his question, J had had no idea, at least on the conscious level, of what "resources of simple humanity" he was going to suggest, but now a plan leaped full-grown into his mind. "Remember Zoe Cornwall?"

Leighton frowned. "I seem to have heard the name somewhere."

"Dash it, man! She was the woman Richard was engaged to, around the time our experiments first began. He had to break off with her because of our damned official security."

"Yes, I think it's coming to me. She got married, as I recall, to some accountant."

J began pacing again. "That's right. Reginald Smythe-Evans, C.P.A. That's the chap. A decent enough fellow, though of course Richard never could stomach him. Richard and I and a few other lads from MI6A were playing hide and seek with the Russians at her wedding. Damn poor form on our part, but we were desperate. She forgave him, and in fact made him second-godfather of her third child."

Leighton said wistfully, "Her third child. God, how the years fly by."

J pressed on with growing excitement. "Richard has had many women since then, both here in England and in various X dimensions, but it has always been my impression that Zoe has remained for him *the* woman, as Conan Doyle might have put it. With all the others Richard has held something back, knowing that the relationship could not last. Only with Zoe had he even the illusion that a life-long proper Church-of-England marriage was possible."

"Come to the point, man," Leighton snapped.

"The point is this: Zoe may be the one thing in the whole world Richard has not forgotten. If he could see her again, it could jog his memory, start him on the road to recovery."

Leighton stroked his chin thoughtfully with a small hand. "Hmm. You may have something there, but if she's a happily married woman, would it be wise to, as it were, blow on the fading embers?"

38

"I won't ask her to divorce her husband or anything like that, of course. What's done is done. I only want Richard to see her, to speak to her if he can speak, or listen to her if he can't. How can she refuse a request for a single visit? For a few hours of her time? Once Richard meant a great deal to her, you know. He still does, if I'm any judge."

"Do you know where she is?"

"No, but I can find her. MI6 can find anyone it really wants to find."

The scientist nodded slowly. "I'd forgotten you were the original Great Octopus, but before you pick up the telephone and start slithering your tentacles out through the wires, perhaps you should consider that you may be placing this lady in grave danger."

"Danger? What do you mean?" J had started toward the telephone on the desk, but now he paused.

"Nobody knows the limits of this creature's powers, this thing from who knows where. If Richard's old flame can actually threaten our Mr. Thing in any way, as we certainly hope she can, Mr. Thing may take steps to defend himself. For all we know Mr. Thing is in this room listening to us at this very moment."

J glanced uneasily around. "Nonsense. You told me yourself the thing was still contained within the hospital and computer complex." He picked up the receiver of the old-fashioned desk phone and dialed Copra House.

Ten minutes later, his call completed, J hung up and turned to face Lord Leighton.

"You'll like a happy man," Leighton commented, smiling. "It does your soul good, doesn't it, to do something, anything, even if it's the wrong thing?"

"It's not the wrong thing." J walked slowly to the window and looked out. It may have been imagination, but the overcast sky seemed markedly brighter. Was that a touch of green on the branch of one of the leafless trees in Prince's Gate Crescent?

J glanced down.

On the sidewalk, gazing up at him with an expression that was, at one and the same time, shy and bold, innocent and challenging, stood a girl, not more than ten years old. Her clothing—a short skirt, sweater, bobby socks and saddle shoes—was curiously out of style, and she wore her blonde hair in a pony tail.

At first J was about to grin at her with the vacant grin he

reserved for all small children who insisted on being noticed by him, then the thought entered his mind, *Are you Jane Colby?*

The girl answered his unspoken question with a teasing nod.

"Leighton," said J softly. "Come here, quickly."

Before the hunchback could limp to the window, Jane Colby had skipped on down the sidewalk and out of sight.

Chapter 4

The bells in the massive tower of the Church of Saint Peter Mancroft in Norwich had ceased pealing, but their humming drone had not yet faded away to silence when a pale slender woman in her thirties emerged from the Royal Shopping Arcade, crossed Gentleman's Walk, and entered the wide market area in the center of town, moving slowly through the crowd, stopping here and there at the stalls to buy fruit and vegetables. She wore a yellow plastic raincoat and hat, as did the three boys of various ages who tagged along behind her, for it had recently rained and the cold breeze and overcast sky promised more rain soon.

"Mama, let me carry it." This was the youngest who piped up, stretching his arms to accept the bag of apples she had purchased.

"All right, Dickie." She carefully handed it to him.

Mrs. Zoe Cornwall Smythe-Evans smiled. Dickie was not like his older brothers. He had a surprising maturity, a manliness, an almost knightly chivalry the others lacked, and there was no denying he was healthier, and that he was stronger than the others had been at his age. While the others moped about, doing as little as possible, little Dickie was always springing forward to volunteer his services. What could be the cause of the difference?

All three boys had the same father; the eldest was named Reggie Jr., and the next younger called Smitty, both taking their identities from Reginald Smythe-Evans. Dickie had many names. He was christened Edward Thomas Richard Smythe-Evans, but somehow from the beginning she could only think of him as Dickie, the name he had gotten from his second-godfather, Richard Blade. Had the name influenced her in some subliminal way, making her expect more of him than of the others, and had the child sensed this expectation and responded to it? She did not know, but this was not the first time the idea had crossed her mind.

Packing a head of lettuce into her string bag and paying the mustached vendor, she let her thoughts slip back into the past, to the days and the nights she'd spent with Richard at his seaside cottage in Dorset so many, many years ago. It was amazing how vividly those memories came back to her at times, though for the most part her busy life occupied her full attention, allowing little time for daydreams.

Her wild-set dark eyes clouded. Her generous mouth formed into a frown. She did not like to think of Richard. There was pain in the memories as well as pleasure, and frustration, and a curiosity that did not fade with the years, but grew gradually stronger. What was the secret work Richard had never been able to tell her about, the work that had finally destroyed their plans for a life together? Was he some sort of secret agent, or a criminal, or something else, something so strange as to be entirely outside her experience?

Richard Blade!

Against her will she saw his rugged face again, heard his voice, felt his touch, and was transported to a time—one time among many—when he and she had drifted in the gentle rise and fall of the breathing surf and watched the sunrise.

"Damn you, Dick," she whispered.

"What?" asked little Dickie, surprised and worried.

"Nothing, Dickie. I was thinking of someone else."

The boy was visibly relieved, yet there remained in his eyes that terrible alertness, the same alertness she had often seen in the dark restless eyes of his namesake.

Her shopping done, she left the marketplace, crossed the narrow road called Gaol Hill, and passed the brooding ancient flintstone Guildhall that stood like a medieval sentinel guarding the northern boundary of the city square.

Here the crowd thinned out and she quickened her pace so that Dickie, with his short legs, was forced to trot. The other boys lounged along sullenly, plainly resentful at having their precious time wasted on a boring shopping expedition. Though they were big enough to help, Zoe had not been able to bring herself to ask them to carry anything. Reggie would have answered, echoing his father, "We have servants to do the bleedin' shopping."

Except for little Dickie, who now stumped cheerfully along at her side, nobody in her social circle could understand her need to do things for herself, even if they were things that "weren't done." All of them sat down most of the time, and smoked a great deal, and drank a great deal in a quiet way

42

and tried to look world-weary. Their favorite expression was, "You'll get over it, my dear." If she showed any feeling at all, any unusual happiness or unhappiness, someone would always parrot, "You'll get over it, my dear."

She sometimes thought, *How efficient! A single bit of wisdom that fits every possible occasion!* She'd never been able to bring herself to say the loathsome phrase, even on those occasions when it really did fit.

Sometimes her friends asked her, "Are you happy?"

She would answer, "I suppose so."

It always satisfied them to hear her say that.

She strode along narrow Dove Street, crossed Pottergate, and continued on to the corner of Duke Street and Charing Cross, passing under the overhanging second floors of the ancient pastel-painted cottages. There she paused to let Reggie and Smitty catch up. They had been dawdling along behind, listlessly trying to push each other into the gutter.

"Mama," Dickie said suddenly. "Do I know him?"

"Know who?" she asked, puzzled.

"The man you're mad it. The man with my name."

"No you don't, dear."

"Will I ever meet him?"

She shook her head firmly. "Never! Now let's hurry home. Daddy will worry about us if we're out when the rain starts." She had already felt a few tiny droplets on her cheek.

The rain began in earnest as they came in through the garden gate, so Zoe and the boys were forced to run the last few hundred yards along the stone walkway, up the red brick steps, across the little porch and, with a whoop of laughter from Zoe and Dickie, through the tall front doorway into the vestibule. Reggie and Smitty ran, but they permitted themselves no laughter, only a mild annoyance.

The Smythe-Evans residence was, to judge by its exterior, a beautiful old house, as beautiful and as old as any of the others in the neighborhood, half-timbered, tile-roofed, vaguely Tudor, with the stucco portions of the wall in a pale candylike "Suffolk pink." It was surrounded with the usual trees, the usual flowers, and the usual lawns.

The interior, however, had been modernized by Reginald's father some time in the Roaring Twenties, and the omnipresent Art Deco furniture and hangings were not yet old enough to be quaint, but too old to make a strong statement in favor of progress.

Mrs. Kelly, the roly-poly cleaning woman, paused on her way down the hall stairs to frown disapprovingly as Zoe opened the closet and proceeded to put her yellow raincoat on a hanger.

"May I be assisting you, mum?" the old woman demanded.

"No, thank you, Mrs. Kelly. I can manage." Zoe was helping the children off with their coats.

"There was a telephone call for you, mum."

"Really? Who from?"

"I've no idea, mum. When I found out it was long distance, I passed the phone to the mister."

"If you don't know who it was from, surely you can tell me *where* it was from."

"From London, mum."

"London? I don't know anyone in London. At least, not anymore."

Mrs. Kelly drew herself up indignantly. "I wouldn't lie to you, mum."

"No, no, of course you wouldn't." Zoe was perplexed.

The children, freed from their raincoats, clambered up the stairs. Mrs. Kelly, with a minimum of movement, stood aside to let them pass.

From the library, at the opposite end of the entrance hall, came the well-modulated, profoundly civilized voice of "the mister" himself, Reginald Smythe-Evans. "Is that you, dear?"

"Yes. I'm home," Zoe answered brightly.

"Could you come in here for a moment, old girl?" In his carefully controlled tone there was a trace of tension that only someone who knew him well could have detected.

"Of course." She hurried to the library door and opened it.

Reginald, behind his massive plain "functionally modern" desk, looked up at her as she entered. He was pale, thin, balding, and had a spotty complexion. He forced a broad toothy grin as he leaned back in his chair, but the illusion of ease and calm was spoiled by the way he pulled nervously at the lapels of his brown tweed suitcoat with his long white fingers. To her surprise, she noticed beads of sweat on his forehead.

"Good Lord, Reggie. What's the matter?"

"If you'll sit down, I'll tell you." He gestured toward one of the few chairs in the room. (It was, she knew, no more uncomfortable than any of the others.)

She sat down, saying, "The phone call?"

44

"Yes."

"What was it?"

"You remember that fellow Richard Blade?"

"Blade?"

"Come, come, old girl. I know you remember him. I daresay there are times when you're out of sorts with me that you wish you were his wife instead of mine. I'm not a fool, you know." He paused, frowning. "But be that as it may, it seems something's happened to him."

"Happened? Are you trying to tell me he's dead?"

Reginald waved the suggestion aside with a languid hand. "No, nothing like that. His employer, a chap named Jay, claims your Mr. Blade is sick. Yes, and it seems the only thing can put the fellow to rights is a few words from you. Bleeding romantic, eh what?"

"Reggie, there's no need to be upset. Whatever there was between Richard Blade and me is over."

"Nothing but memories, eh? Never mind. I'm not the sort to turn up on the front page of *The Sun,* a smoking revolver in my hand and my wife and her lover tastefully piled in the background."

Impulsively she stood up and leaned over to kiss him lightly on the cheek, whispering, "You do understand me, don't you?"

"Yes. Quite. Are you going to see Mr. Blade?"

"Not if you say no."

"I won't be put in the position of jailer, my dear. You're old enough to make up your own mind."

She sat down again, unnerved by the coldness in her husband's voice. "What's the phone number of this Jay person?" she asked. "We could ring him back and see how serious this is. Perhaps there's no real need for me to step in."

"He wouldn't give me his phone number, my dear. If he's Richard Blade's employer, his phone number is probably secret, like everything else about him. He said he would phone back."

She searched her memory frantically. Jay? Jay? Suddenly she placed him. J! The funny old man with no name, only an initial. He'd been at her wedding, hovering in the background, always in the background. Had she known J before? Had she seen him after that? She could not remember. The man was so gray, so utterly—perhaps deliberately—forgettable.

When the telephone on the desk rang, it startled her badly. Though she sprang up and reached for it, Reginald was quicker.

"Hello. Reginald Smythe-Evans speaking. Yes, she's here now."

He handed her the receiver.

J had briskly walked the few blocks from the Tower of London to the Fenchurch Street Station where now he paused inside the entrance, stepping out of the stream of pedestrian traffic to examine his pocketwatch and get his breath.

He was a little early, though the gathering darkness outside in the street showed nightfall was not far off, overcast blurring the distinction between night and day. By fast train, as J knew, Norwich was only two hours from London. Mrs. Smythe-Evans would be arriving in three minutes, if the British railway system performed with its customary punctuality. He waited, composing himself, until he heard, above the murmur of the crowd, the rumble of the train entering the station, then he went to meet her.

He recognized her instantly when he saw her coming toward him along the platform. The years had been remarkably kind to her; at least at a distance she seemed hardly changed at all from the time he had seen her at her wedding. She was wearing a yellow plastic raincoat, unbuttoned in front to reveal a tasteful tweed pantsuit, and she carried a small green overnight bag.

J frowned. At her side strolled her husband in a similar yellow raincoat, and following him, trotting along hand in hand, came three yellow-raincoat-clad boys. Bringing up the rear, in another yellow raincoat, was a fat, red-faced woman, who could only be their maid, loaded down with luggage. Mrs. Smythe-Evans had brought her whole family.

"Damn and blast," J muttered, but he hid his consternation behind a set of shiny grinning false teeth as he advanced to welcome her.

"Ah, Mrs. Smythe-Evans!" He shook her hand heartily. "How good of you to come. And this, I take it, is your husband?"

"Yes. J, meet Reginald Smythe-Evans," she answered brightly.

The men shook hands.

46

Reginald said stiffly, "Jay? Is that your first name or your last?"

"Neither, old man. It's only a nickname, but people have been calling me by it for so long I hardly remember any other." Reginald obviously was not satisfied with this answer, but J turned to the children. "And these, I suppose, are your handsome children?"

"That's right," she replied, somewhat nervously, but with a note of pride in her voice. "Here's Reggie Jr., and Smitty. Shake hands with the gentleman, boys." Gravely they obeyed. "And this is my youngest, little Dickie." J found a small hand thrust into his, and a pair of dark eyes peering up at him with a look of disquieting intelligence.

"Pleased to meet you, sir," said Dickie.

"I hope you don't mind if I brought my family along," she continued. "I thought if I was coming in to London anyway, we might as well make an event of it. The boys are out of school, and Reggie has been working so hard he deserves a holiday. It's all right, isn't it?" She looked at J doubtfully.

"Of course, of course. No problem," J assured her. "I've booked a room at a hotel for you not far from here, and I'm sure we can expand the reservation to cover your *entourage*. If you'll follow me . . . " He led the way toward the exit, allowing no trace of his inner indignation to show outwardly.

"Perhaps I can be of some assistance with this Blade business," Reginald offered, falling in step.

"I'm afraid not, old chap," J said.

"I can come along for moral support, at least," Reginald persisted.

"Thank you, but I'll have to say no." J was firm.

"And why not?" Reginald demanded.

Awkwardly J explained, "It's a matter of security, classified information, government secrets and all that rot. I don't make the rules, but I have to play by them. Your wife is cleared—that is, she has a security clearance."

"And I don't?" said Reginald.

"That's right."

Now Reginald was genuinely surprised. "Why should she have a clearance when I don't?"

J hesitated a moment, then told him the truth. "When your wife was, so to speak, intimately associated with our Richard Blade, we looked into her background quite carefully, and we've kept track of her, in our quiet way, ever since. Strictly routine, you understand, but fortunate in this case.

47

That's how we were able to find her so easily. I'm sure you're a loyal British subject, Mr. Smythe-Evans, at least as loyal as Kim Philby or some other people who have gotten the highest clearances only to turn out to be Russian spies. Obviously this security clearance business doesn't work. Obviously it only makes us keep tripping over our own feet, but it's a tradition. You can't expect us to go against tradition."

"I suppose not," Reginald reluctantly agreed, bewildered but clearly impressed by the cloak-and-dagger atmosphere J had managed to project.

"I'll get you all settled in your hotel," J said in a business-like tone. "Then I'll borrow your wife for a few hours. I hate to inconvenience you, but it's dreadfully important. You can fend for yourself for awhile, can't you?"

"I suppose so."

J clapped him on the back. "There's a good chap!"

They came out of the station and descended the steps into Hart Street, hunching their shoulders against the chill of early evening.

Chapter 5

The Tower of London had been officially closed for hours. The quaint red-uniformed Yeomen Warders who squired the tourists during the day and served, in their way, as guards had long since left. The only people who remained were the inconspicuous plainclothesmen of MI6A who hovered around the entrance as if waiting for an omnibus that never came.

As J and Zoe trudged across the street, two of the agents came forward into the pale illumination of the streetlamp to meet them.

"Good evening, sir," said the taller. "Identification, please."

J handed over his papers.

"And the lady, sir?" the other asked.

"Her name is Zoe Smythe-Evans," J said.

She showed the man her driver's license. He frowned, dissatisfied.

"I'll take full responsibility for her," J added.

The taller man took J to one side and said softly, "This is highly irregular, sir."

"I know that."

The agent shrugged. "Very well, sir. Password?"

"Lotus."

"Countersign Eaters," said the man, snapping on his flashlight.

"Follow me, please."

While his partner remained behind, the tall man led J and Zoe through the deserted Tower Park, among the ancient cannons and leafless trees. There was no fog tonight, and J could see the lights on the opposite bank of the river, and their reflections shimmering in the water like ghostly spears of colored flame. Ahead and above, endless streams of headlights crossed the massive Tower Bridge.

The agent unlocked the Traitor's Gate and let J and Zoe in, then left them to continue on their own. Zoe exclaimed with surprise when J opened the hidden door. "Amazing! I could have sworn that was a blank wall."

J chuckled and continued on.

Zoe followed though it was plain she found the long dim damp tunnel and the maze of subbasements highly distasteful.

When they reached the elevator, Zoe pressed the button.

J smiled when the elevator did not come.

"What's keeping it?" she demanded.

"It doesn't know you, my dear."

J pressed with his thumb, and the elevator arrived an instant later.

"How did you do that?" she asked as she stepped inside.

"Magic, my dear. Magic."

They plunged downward at an alarming speed, then slowed to a stop. "I feel ill," Zoe said softly, long fingers touching the base of her throat.

The door slid open.

In a brilliantly lighted foyer a man behind an olive drab desk looked up from a magazine he was reading. The man wore a green uniform and was armed with a large pistol in a hip holster. He looked at Zoe and frowned.

"We're going down, Peters," said J.

Peters pressed a button on his desk. The elevator door closed. Again they plummeted downward.

Zoe said, "I would rather have gotten off there and taken the stairs."

J answered, "If you had stepped into that foyer, you would have heard more alarm bells, sirens and whistles than you'd care to hear in a lifetime."

"Good Lord. You must be guarding something frightfully valuable in there. What is it?"

"The Russians know there's something in there, but they don't know what it is. I hope you don't expect to be better informed than they are."

The elevator decelerated.

"This will be our little hospital," J said.

"How convenient."

The door slid open.

Standing in the hall, waiting, were Lord Leighton and Dr. Leonard Ferguson. Both looked haggard and tense, as if they had not slept in a long time.

When the introductions had been completed, Dr. Ferguson said, "Come along, dear." The fat little psychiatrist had an oily way with women. Rumor had it, around the project, that he had seduced an awesome number of females, but J had never been able to understand what they saw in the fellow.

Now he was saying, as he waddled along, "You look pale, dear. Are you feeling well?"

"I'm all right, doctor. I was a bit queasy in the lift, but I'm fine now."

"There's a good girl." He patted her arm.

Lord Leighton, hobbling along behind, grunted, "I hope you've prepared her for what she's going to see, J. Yes, Mrs. Smythe-Evans, this could be quite a shock to you. Richard Blade is far from being the man you remember."

"What exactly is wrong with him?" Now that her husband was not around, she made no attempt to conceal her concern.

"Amnesia, with fits of violence," the hunchback answered grimly.

"He probably won't recognize you," Ferguson put in. "In fact, Mrs. Smythe-Evans, I must warn you that I am very pessimistic about this whole business of bringing you here. It smacks a good deal more of the telly than sound psychiatric procedure. Indeed, I probably would have voted against the idea if I'd been given the opportunity to do so."

"It's my idea," J admitted. "If it doesn't work, we'll simply have to think of another one, won't we?"

"And you think seeing me will bring back his memory?" she asked, puzzled.

"Exactly," J said with conviction, a conviction he did not feel.

"I've had Mr. Blade moved to a new room while we—er—redecorate his old one," Ferguson said with a touch of ironic humor J always found so annoying. "Here we are."

They stopped before the closed door of Room 27.

"Are you ready, Mrs. Smythe-Evans?" Ferguson said gently.

She bit her lip and nodded.

Ferguson opened the door.

He hasn't changed.

That was Zoe's first impression as she entered the room and diffidently approached the foot of the bed. Richard Blade's affliction had removed, along with his memory, the facial expression of age, relaxing his muscles, smoothing the lines around his eyes and mouth. For a moment he seemed exactly

51

the big, powerful, yet reserved and gentlemanly fellow he'd been when first they'd met, so many years ago, the man who'd looked like an athlete but had quoted poetry like a Rhodes scholar.

Then she looked again, and felt a chill creep over her. Those dark eyes, which once had been so unnervingly alert, were now dull, unfocused and opaque. And she noticed, with an unpleasant jolt, that he was strapped down to the bed.

Dr. Ferguson spoke to the burly white-clad orderly who stood nearby. "Have you discontinued sedation?"

"Yes, sir." The man looked worried.

"Good," Ferguson said thoughtfully. "We want the poor fellow to be able to react if he can."

"But I'm ready with the tranquilizer if he gets wild." The orderly indicated a large dart pistol on the dresser.

"Acetylcholine esterase?"

"Yes, sir."

Ferguson nodded with satisfaction. "Good. The barbiturate charge we used before was a little slow."

Zoe continued to stare into Richard Blade's tanned empty face. "Can he see me?" she whispered.

"Oh, certainly, if he looks at you," Ferguson assured her.

"Say something to him, Mrs. Smythe-Evans," J prompted.

She leaned forward over the foot of the bed. "Richard?" she called softly.

He did not respond.

"Richard?" she repeated, louder.

Still he gave no sign.

Ferguson shrugged. "I didn't think it would work. We might as well leave poor Mr. Blade in peace and . . . "

"Try again," J commanded sharply, ignoring the fat little psychiatrist. "Try again, Mrs. Smythe-Evans!"

Her vision blurred with sudden tears. "Please," she said. "Please. It's me, Zoe." She moved to Blade's bedside and touched his cheek with her fingertips.

"Be careful, miss," the orderly warned nervously.

"There's no danger," Lord Leighton snapped. "Blade's trussed up like a blooming mummy."

"He's a strong one, he is," said the orderly, still not at all at ease.

"Don't you remember me?" she pleaded. "Dick? Dick? Can't you answer me?" Ineffectually she stroked his dark unruly hair.

Then she felt his head turn toward her and it seemed to

her, through her tears, that she saw a faint trace of a smile on his lips.

"Look out there, miss," said the orderly. "He's moving."

"Moving?" she cried. "He's smiling! Can't you see he's smiling?"

"We mustn't give way to wishful thinking, my dear," Ferguson said, but he had stepped forward and was staring intently at Richard's features. Leighton and J had also come forward.

"You remember me, Dick," she said triumphantly. "I know you do! But you must give some sign for the others. Prove it to them!"

Richard Blade's lips moved.

"Dorset," he whispered.

"What did he say?" Leighton demanded.

"He said Dorset," J answered.

She clutched Blade's shoulders, her fingernails digging into the rough white material of his hospital gown, and said urgently, "You remember Dorset? So do I! Do you remember the cottage, the sea, the cold mornings when I fixed your breakfast? Do you remember how we used to swim together in the surf before dawn? The long walks down those country lanes with all the trees and cows? Do you remember that niche in the cliff top I called 'Blade's Snuggery,' where we made love outdoors and didn't give a damn?" The tears were flowing freely down her cheeks and dropping from her chin onto his bedcovers. "Do you remember how we used to quote poetry to each other?" She paused, sobbing, unable to speak. The vision she was trying to make Richard remember had overwhelmed her, and everything that had happened in the intervening years seemed unreal and dreamlike.

She got a grip on herself, wiped her eyes with the backs of her hands like a child, and began reciting "Dover Beach" by Matthew Arnold in a shaking voice, ignoring Ferguson, J, Lord Leighton and the orderly as if they were not there. This poem, more than any other, they had quoted and re-quoted and sometimes, for fun or in the heat of emotion, misquoted.

The sea is calm tonight,
The tide is full, the moon lies fair
Upon the straits;—on the French coast the light
Gleams and is gone; the cliffs of England stand,
Glimmering and vast, out in the . . .

Richard Blade screamed.

"What's wrong?" Zoe cried, suddenly all concern.

He screamed again, and she thought he was screaming a word, a word she'd never heard before, a word from some unknown ianguage the very sounds of which were alien to any familiar alphabet.

"Ngaa!" he shrieked, his face contorted into a mask of horror. "Ngaa! Ngaa! Ngaa!"

Blade's eyes seemed fixed on some spot above her left shoulder. She turned to look, but there was nothing there.

"Ngaa! Ngaa! Ngaa!"

He began to toss from side to side as much as his fetters would allow.

The orderly snatched up the dart pistol from the dresser. "Back, miss. He's getting violent!"

"Those straps will hold him," Leighton said, but there was uncertainty in his voice.

"Easy there, Mr. Blade. Easy does it. Tell us what you see," Dr. Ferguson said soothingly. "We're all with you. Whatever it is, we won't let it get you."

Abruptly Richard was silent, his eyes now fully alert. His gaze moved swiftly from face to face, taking in the circle of anxious onlookers in an instant.

"That's better," Ferguson said with relief. "We can talk . . . "

Before he could finish his sentence Blade began to strain at his bonds, muscles standing out like cables, face turning red with the effort, beads of sweat standing out on his forehead.

"Stand back, all of you!" shouted the orderly, aiming the pistol with a shaking hand.

"For God's sake, man," Leighton snapped. "Put that toy down. Blade can't get loose." He pushed the weapon aside.

"He can! He can!" insisted the orderly, almost hysterical.

Suddenly one of the straps broke with an explosive pop, then another, and another. Blade took a deep breath, then began straining again, groaning with the effort.

Zoe felt pudgy fingers grip her arm and drag her away. Ferguson muttered, "Come along, dear. Quickly!"

J and Leighton, on either side of her, were retreating too.

The orderly took aim and squeezed the trigger. There was a sharp snicking sound and the dart, fired at point blank range, buried itself in Richard Blade's shoulder. With a roar of wordless rage, Blade thrashed free of his upper restraints. Only his legs remained bound.

The orderly fired again.

Blade fell back on his left elbow, an expression of surprise on his face.

"Get help, doctor," the orderly said hoarsely.

"Right away," Ferguson answered, backing out the door. He was still clutching Zoe's arm in a painful grip, hauling her with him whether she liked it or not.

J and Leighton were not far behind.

Ferguson punched the button on an intercom in the hall and shouted into it, "Orderlies to Room Twenty-seven! Orderlies to Room Twenty-seven! On the double! Emergency! Every available man to Room Twenty-seven!"

In the room, Blade was subsiding, his movements becoming more sluggish, his expression more blank and emotionless; yet still he seemed to be staring at something hovering above him near the ceiling.

Zoe said brokenly, "Poor Dick. Frightened to death of something that isn't there."

J laughed mirthlessly. "We couldn't see it, but there was something there, all right. Make no mistake about that!"

The public address system pinged and the dispatcher took up the call, "Orderlies to Room Twenty-seven. Orderlies to Room Twenty-seven. Emergency."

Zoe caught one more glimpse of Blade, now lying quietly, eyes fixed on . . . something, then the orderlies stampeded past her into the room and slammed the door behind them.

Chapter 6

Upon arriving back at her hotel room, Zoe found that her family was not there. She had a few minutes of anxiety before she found Reginald's note propped against the clock radio on the bedtable.

Zoe darling,
  Mrs. Kelly and I have taken the children to the cinema. We should return some time between midnight and one.
                                          Love,
                                          Reggie.

She sighed. Reginald knew that was way past the children's bedtime. Reggie Jr. and Smitty would be fretful and unmanageable tomorrow, though Dickie would undoubtedly bear up like the little soldier he was. *Reginald's revenge*, she thought.

Reginald's revenges were like that; a subtle blend of pettiness and cunning. If she tried to point an accusing finger at him, he could always say, "Why, I never dreamed you'd mind," or "I meant no harm," or "Don't be paranoid."

Reginald did not like her seeing Richard Blade, not even under the present circumstances, where the man's sanity hung in the balance, but he would never be so old-fashioned and overbearing as to forbid her.

She thought, *I wonder what his next revenge will be?* She knew from experience that more sly, petty, intangible punishments lay ahead.

She glanced at the digital dial of the clock radio. It was past one already. What was Reginald up to? She suspected something sticky, something fundamentally sticky. Would he keep the children up until dawn, then come breezing in with some remark like, "I thought that once in their lives they should see the sun come up over London." Yes, that was his style exactly.

But no, now she heard their cheerful voices down the hall.

56

All was well. She heaved a mighty sigh of relief as she sat down on the edge of the wide and luxurious bed, and a moment later the key turned in the lock and Reginald, all smiles, opened the door to let in three weary but happy boys and one grim Irishwoman.

"Well, dear," he said, bending to give her a peck on the cheek. " Did you cure him?"

"No," she answered wistfully. "I think I made him worse."

Mrs. Kelly was about to herd the children into the connecting suite when Zoe turned to speak to them. "Did you enjoy the film, boys?"

"Oh, yes!" answered round-eyed Dickie.

"I've seen better," said Reggie Jr.

"Bleeding tacky, I thought," grumbled Smitty.

"What sort of film was it?" Zoe asked brightly.

"A monster film," said Dickie with awe.

"A tacky bleeding dinosaur went about stepping on extras," said Reggie Jr. with disgust.

"I could tell he wasn't real," added Smitty.

"I thought he was grand, Mama," Dickie said, not at all discouraged by his brothers' "higher criticism."

"All children love monsters," Reginald said, grinning.

"Speak for yourself, Dad," said Reggie Jr.

"He was grand, Mama," Dickie repeated. "Bigger than a churchtower!" He came over to her and she gave him a hug.

"They found a little friend, you know," Reginald said. "There was a girl in the cinema. She sat next to Dickie and kept whispering things to him. Very odd. She couldn't have been more than twelve years old, but there wasn't a sign of her parents."

"What did she tell you, Dickie?" Zoe inquired.

"Oh Mama, she said all kinds of awful things. She said she was from another world, and that she was going to make slaves of everyone by getting into their minds. She said she had hundreds and hundreds of brothers and sisters back home where she came from, and that they were all coming to London to get into our minds." She could tell Dickie was upset but hiding his feelings.

Mrs. Kelly snorted, "Sure and it's trashy films like this one put such ideas into the lassy's head, mum. You and the mister should have a care what you let the youngsters see, or one day they'll be spoutin' the same nonsense, and running around to one theater after another in the middle of the night all by theirselves."

"Come, come," said Reginald. "No harm done."

But Zoe, with her arm around Dickie's shoulders, could feel the boy trembling. "Did the dinosaur scare you, Dickie?" she asked him.

"No, mama. It was the girl. The dinosaur was grand."

"Bedtime, lads," Mrs. Kelly said impatiently.

"Mama," Dickie said, "The girl said she was going to kill people, lots of people."

"So long as it isn't us," Reginald said smugly. "Now run along to bed, the lot of you."

Dickie had more to say, but Reginald and Mrs. Kelly hurried him along into the next room with his brothers. Reginald was undoing his tie as he returned.

"I suppose we'll be on our way back to Norwich tomorrow night," he said.

"I should stay awhile, dear. They may need me," Zoe answered.

"We can all stay then."

"No, at least the children should go home."

"And me?" He took off his suitcoat and carefully put it on a hanger.

"Do as you wish. Mrs. Kelly is quite able to care for the boys without your help."

"I will remain in London then." He unbuttoned his shirt.

"To keep an eye on me?"

"Nonsense. You are a lady. I have every confidence you'll behave like one. I have certain matters of business to take care of in the metropolis, and this is an excellent opportunity to see to them, that's all. Yes, Mrs. Kelly can take the children back to Norwich, and you and I will stay here. I only hope this Blade chap recovers quickly. Hotel rooms aren't cheap, you know."

"J has assured me our room and board will be paid by the government."

"That settles it! We'll be able to get back at least a small part of all that money we've paid in taxes. Where are my pajamas, old girl?"

"In the black suitcase," she answered listlessly.

Once in bed, with the lights out, Reginald dozed off almost immediately. Zoe however, in spite of her weariness and the lateness of the hour, lay awake, staring at the ceiling and listening to the murmur of the city.

She thought, *Will morning never come?*

Then, little by little, she became aware of an unpleasant sensation, as if she were being watched, as if someone were in the room. She tried to ignore it, but the sensation grew steadily stronger until she could localize it in the space at the foot of her bed. She looked in that direction but could see nothing, at least in the dim light that filtered in through the drawn curtains at the window. There was a redness in the light that blinked on and off rhythmically, suggesting a neon sign outside somewhere.

She thought, *There's no one there. I'm imagining things.*

Reginald rolled onto his back and began to snore. His snoring, which ordinarily annoyed her, was now curiously reassuring. She was tempted to awaken him in order to have someone to talk to, someone to drive away the phantoms of her imagination, but she didn't have the heart. Poor Reginald needed his sleep.

She thought, *I'm upset over what's happened to Richard, that's all.* Thinking of Richard brought a sudden rush of tenderness and concern that surprised her. Why did she feel this way about a man she had known so briefly, had never known well, so long ago? Futile feelings! Even if Richard recovered, nothing would be changed. Richard would have his work—his secret, secret work she could never share or even know about—and she would have Reginald and the children.

She remembered a line from Fitzgerald's "Rubaiyat of Omar Khayyam."

"The moving finger writes, and having writ moves on."

Suddenly, from the foot of her bed, a voice whispered her name.

"Zoe?"

She sat bolt upright, peering into the gloom, startled yet not frightened. The bodiless voice had sounded friendly, familiar. She had heard that voice somewhere before.

After a long pause, the voice spoke again, softly. "The tide is full, the moon lies fair upon the straits."

She recognized the quote from "Dover Beach." More important, she recognized the voice.

"Richard?" she called gently.

There was no answer.

She waited a long time, but there was nothing more to hear but the ordinary drone of London's night sounds.

Being careful not to wake Reginald, she slipped out of bed

and silently dressed, thinking, *I'll go for a walk in the streets. Then the voice will be able to speak to me without disturbing Reginald.*

Still she felt no fear. The voice had been Richard's. She was not afraid of Richard. This must have something to do with Richard's secret work. A new kind of radio, perhaps.

She took the room key and let herself out, then walked briskly down the harshly lit hallway to the elevator.

She had seen the Tower Bridge and the Thames and the rumbling lorries full of produce for London's markets. She had seen the drunken ragged derelicts shuffling somnambulistically from doorway to doorway; one had roused himself from his stupor to stare at her, amazed to see a "lady of quality" out alone at night. She had seen the sky grow brighter as dawn approached.

She had not seen Richard Blade, or heard his voice again, nor had she felt his unseen presence as before. The world, to her bitter disappointment, had returned to normal.

The only excitement in her wanderings had been a moment when police cars and fire engines had rushed past her, traveling in the opposite direction and making a dreadful din. She had paid no attention to them.

As she made her way back to her hotel by a circuitous route, she smelled smoke and heard the distant clamor of excited voices, but these things too she ignored.

Until she rounded a corner and saw, two blocks away, her own hotel besieged by firemen, great gouts of oily black smoke belching from its windows.

"My God," she whispered, and broke into a run.

Panting, wild-haired, she collided with the crowd that had gathered, even at this early hour, to watch the disaster. "Let me through!" she shouted. "My children are in that building!" She fought her way into the mob, pushing aside people who pushed back angrily, cursing and swearing at her. She had almost reached the line of grim-faced policemen who blocked the bystanders' advance when a man appeared ahead of her and called, "Mrs. Smythe-Evans?"

"Yes! Yes! I'm Mrs. Smythe-Evans!"

"You probably don't recognize me but . . . "

She did recognize him. He was the tall plainclothesman who had been guarding the entrance to the secret project in the Tower of London. She shoved through to him and grabbed him by the arm. "What is it? Tell me!" she cried.

He was pale in the predawn light. "We had your room under routine surveillance, you know. J's orders. And there was a man following you on your walk, though you probably didn't notice." He was obviously stalling, putting off telling her something. "Well, you see, the fire broke out in your rooms. It was an explosion, like an incendiary bomb. I was in the room across the hall. Barely got out in time myself."

"What are you saying?" she demanded. "My family? Were they . . . ?"

"I'm sorry, Mrs. Smythe-Evans," he said miserably. "Your children, your husband, your maid . . . I don't see how any of them could have escaped alive."

The wind shifted and a cloud of black smoke engulfed her, acrid, stinging, foul, choking her, blinding her, throwing her into a fit of uncontrollable coughing. She fell against the man, clutched his overcoat sleeves to keep from falling as the tears streamed down her cheeks. He was coughing too, but he managed to keep his balance and hold her up. Policemen were shouting to get back, get back.

The wind shifted again.

She still could not see, but she could speak after a fashion. "Dickie!" she croaked in a hoarse rasping whisper. "Dickie! Dickie!"

Chapter 7

J pressed the rewind button, waited a moment, then pressed first the stop, then the play. For the fifteenth time the cassette player began again. A peculiar animal-like wheeze and snort issued from the loudspeaker.

"Reginald's snore," J commented.

Lord Leighton nodded abstractedly.

"Our agent is to be commended," J said. "It took considerable presence of mind to think of snatching that cassette and taking it with him when the building was bursting into flames around him."

"Yes," Leighton said, but the little hunchback's mind was obviously elsewhere.

J and Leighton had locked themselves into one of the electronics laboratories near the central KALI unit to discuss the morning's hotel fire and what they should do next. The two men were seated, in the diffused bluish light of the overhead fluorescent tubes, on either side of a black enameled-steel table on which rested the recorder, a delicate machine no bigger than a portable typewriter though it reproduced sound as well as all but the most elaborate stereos.

J went through his usual ceremony of lighting his pipe, the beloved dropstem his doctors assured him would sooner or later kill him, then puffed meditatively as the recorded snore continued. When all was well J could go for weeks without a smoke, but when the tension was too great he always relapsed.

On the tape there was a rustling.

"Reginald's waking up," J said, exhaling a cloud of pungent blue smoke.

"Yes," said Leighton.

From the recorder came Reginald's grunt of surprise.

"He must have noticed Mrs. Smythe-Evans was not with him," J said.

Reginald was grumbling now in a low voice, but J could not make out what he was saying. The bedsprings creaked. There was the pad of bare feet crossing a carpet. A door opened. There was the rustle of clothing.

"He's at the closet, putting on his bathrobe," said J.

Reginald said distinctly, "Where has that woman gone?" He sounded angry and suspicious.

"Here comes the knock at the door," J predicted.

On the tape the knock sounded once, twice, three times. "Who can that be?" Reginald muttered. He crossed the room, his footsteps passing close to the hidden microphone. Reginald opened the hall door. J noted that Zoe had left it unlocked.

Reginald said, surprised, "What do you want, little girl?"

J leaned forward. No, the girl did not speak. J would have given a lot to hear her voice.

"Listen to this, Leighton," snapped J.

Abruptly Reginald cried out, "My God! Your hand! It's on fire!"

Then came the roar of flame, a rushing, whooshing roar like a giant blast furnace—then silence.

J pressed the stop button. "Want to hear it again, Lord Leighton?"

"No, that's quite enough, thank you," the scientist said.

J turned off the machine, saying, "I've known you a long time, Leighton. There's something you're keeping from me. I can sense it."

Reluctantly Leighton nodded. "You're right, of course. But before I tell you, I want you to promise me something."

"What?"

"Promise me you won't destroy KALI."

J studied the little man intently before saying softly, "You have my word."

"And another thing."

"Yes?"

"Don't tell the Prime Minister what I'm about to tell you, at least not yet."

"Very well."

Leighton sighed, avoiding J's eyes. "Richard Blade had another of his fits early this morning. He got completely free of his fetters and smashed his bed into scrap iron, all the while screaming that word, 'Ngaa, Ngaa, Ngaa.' He kicked down his locked door and was some distance down the hall before the attendants could knock him out with the tranquilizer guns. I think our boy is developing an immunity to the drugs."

"I don't see . . . "

Leighton raised a hand for silence, then went on. "Here's the point. His fit took place at exactly the same moment the fire started in Mrs. Smythe-Evans's hotel room."

"Coincidence."

"Really? What if I tell you that at that exact same moment, KALI turned itself on."

J took his pipe from his mouth. "Turned itself on? How is that possible?"

"KALI is not like its predecessors. With KALI I've made the final step from manual control to full automation."

"But surely there must be a man to push program start."

Leighton shook his head. "No, not really. KALI can start itself. And it did so this morning."

"Only because some human being put that into its program."

Again the scientist shook his head. "That's not so. I believe I must explain something to you, something I assumed you knew all along, though now I see you haven't grasped it. From the beginning we've talked of first generation computers, second generation computers, third generation computers. Do you know what that means?"

J shrugged. "Something like model A, B, and C."

A bitter smile appeared on Leighton's thin lips. "If only that were all. A second generation computer is programmed by a first generation computer, a third generation computer is programmed by a second generation computer, and so on."

"You mean that KALI has been programmed by another computer, which in turn has been . . . "

"I see you understand."

"How many generations is KALI removed from a human programmer, Leighton?"

"Seventy-five."

"My God," J said softly.

"KALI is far more complex than any human brain. No human brain can think as fast or as well. No human brain can hope, by any amount of study, to understand KALI. KALI has moved into a whole new order of magnitude. A cat or a dog can watch me at my workbench constructing an electric component, but the poor animal can never actually understand what I'm doing no matter how much he sniffs and paws. KALI's mind is to ours as ours is to an animal's! KALI's actions must remain forever a mystery to us because of the biological limitations built into us."

"So all we can do with KALI is sniff and paw?"

"That's right."

"There is one more thing we can do. We can pull the plug."

"That is the one thing we must not do, my dear J."

"Really? Why not?" J returned his pipe to his mouth and discovered it had gone out.

"The sort of thing that has been happening—the poltergeist phenomena, the voices, the haunting, if you will—sometimes happens without KALI's aid. I think the thing that came through KALI with Richard can sometimes manifest itself in our world without KALI's aid, though in a weaker form. Without KALI this thing Richard seems to call a Ngaa can reach us, but only with KALI's aid can we reach it."

J relit his pipe and began to pace the room. "Damn. There's something in what you say, old boy. KALI is not like other computers. It's a computer linked to a human mind, drawing on the powers of both, including powers that ordinarily lie dormant, powers we might almost term supernatural. There was a Yank author—some called him the father of psychic research—named Charles Fort. In the early years of out century he wrote a book called *Wild Talents* in which he advanced the theory that poltergeist phenomena were caused by mental abilities we all possess, but which become active only if something, such as a powerful repressed emotion, provides our psyche with a special stimulation. Fort gathered an awesome mass of data to back up his idea, and it's dogma now to some of the leading psychic research societies. If Fort is right, KALI is not the gate through which the Ngaa enters our dimension. Richard Blade is the gate!"

The hunchback was silent a moment, his yellow-rimmed eyes unfocused, his wide forehead wrinkled in thought. At last he said, "It fits, J. When poor Dexter was taken to Scotland, the Ngaa went with him. It didn't stay here, as it would have done if it had been linked to the computer." He thumped his small bony fist on the tabletop. "By Jove, I believe we are on the verge of a breakthrough."

J halted his pacing and stared gloomily down at the scientist. "Perhaps so, Lord Leighton. We could use one! Do you realize how pitifully little we have learned about the X dimension with all our experiments, with all the time and money we've spent, with all the risks we've taken? Human beings have died and gone mad in our experiments, and what have we to show for it? Richard Blade has gone somewhere, but where?"

Leighton stared at the floor. "I have no idea. At the beginning I was full of pat explanations, but now . . . "

"He has brought back things," J persisted, emphasizing his points with swift stabbing motions of his pipestem. "Things as big as a bathtub and a horse, and things made of materials so alien our best scientists have been unable to duplicate them. Where did these things come from?"

"I don't know," Leighton admitted.

"And surely you've noticed the same mysterious anomalies I have in the stories Richard has related to us under hypnosis during his debriefings. Somehow he always seems to be able to speak the language of any dimension he enters without a single lesson. How can our supercomputers accomplish such a miracle?"

"I don't know." There was an undertone of anguish in Leighton's voice.

"And have you noticed how each and every one of those alien dimensions seemed like a curiously distorted reflection of some era of our own known history? Celtic Britain. Ancient Rome. Feudal Japan. By God Leighton, where is this machine sending him? Backward in time? To some planet in another star system? To a parallel timetrack where society has evolved in a slightly different way? To a future so distant England has been completely forgotten? Where, Leighton, where?"

"I don't know," Leighton repeated hopelessly.

J gestured in the direction of the room where KALI stood, waiting. "Could it be that Richard never leaves that room?"

"What?" Leighton looked up, startled.

"Could it be that those X dimensions are actually fantastically complex simulations existing *within the computer*? Could it be that all of Richard's adventures are built up out of bits and pieces of his own subconscious and given an illusion of reality by the computer?"

"It can't be merely an illusion," Leighton objected. "Richard's body vanishes while he's gone."

"Hundreds of people vanish every year, and even MI6 can't track them down, except for those who surface a few months later in Moscow with a briefcase full of top secret

66

blueprints. The strange thing is not that he vanishes, but that he reappears."

"If he reappears, the X dimensions must be real!" Leighton spoke with the air of a man grasping at straws.

"Unless Richard Blade is disintegrated into his component atoms and stored as bits of information in KALI's memory banks, then reconstituted with appropriate wounds and souvenirs after a suitable period of time, complete with implanted false memories of adventures that never happened. Can KALI do that?"

Stricken, Lord Leighton could only repeat, "I don't know."

J began pacing again. "One thing we can be thankful for. If the Ngaa follows the same pattern this time as it did when it came through the computer with Dexter, we can expect the power of the creatures to gradually dwindle."

"I wouldn't count on that," Leighton said bleakly.

"Why not?"

"This time, when KALI turned itself on, something came through it."

"What do you mean, 'something'?"

"I didn't see it, though I was in the room at the time, but it was recorded on our instruments. I can show you the graphs if . . . "

"Never mind the graphs, Leighton. Tell me, in plain words. What was it?"

In the blue-white fluorescent light Leighton's face was that of a dead man. "It was pure energy, J, the equivalent of hundreds of thousands of volts of electricity."

On stepping out of the elevator, J was met by Dr. Ferguson. Ferguson wore an even more flamboyantly floral Hawaiian sport shirt than before, but there was nothing flamboyant about the fat man's bloodshot, haunted eyes.

"How is Mrs. Smythe-Evans?" J asked.

"She's taking it well," the psychiatrist answered. "The woman's got courage. I offered her something to get her over the rough spots, but she turned me down."

"May I visit her?"

"I don't see why not. She's lying down, but I don't think she's asleep. At least she wasn't when I looked in on her a half-hour ago. Room Eight, that way." He indicated the direction with a weary gesture.

As J started down the hall, Ferguson fell in step beside him,

67

saying, "The poltergeist nonsense has started again, you know, worse than ever. I thought it would die down if we waited long enough, but . . . " He shrugged.

"What happened?"

"Something picked up the filing cabinet in my office and threw it through the wall out into the passage. And did Leighton tell you things have been smashing themselves upstairs too, near KALI?"

"No, he kept quiet about that. He thinks that if I know how serious things have gotten, I'll take his wonderful electric toy away from him."

"A capital idea, I'd say! I hope you do exactly that."

"I don't plan to."

"Why not, in God's name?"

"I want to try something else, first."

"Do something, J! Anything! I'm supposed to be the great healer around here, but I'm about ready for a trip to Scotland myself."

They halted outside Room Eight.

J said, "Unless I'm greatly mistaken, you'll have peace in this place tomorrow morning."

Staring at J with unconcealed disbelief, the doctor opened the door. "A visitor, Mrs. Smythe-Evans," he called with a false cheerfulness.

"Bring him in." Her voice sounded tired.

In the doorway J said, "I hope I'm not intruding. If you'd like to rest . . . "

"I can't sleep. I might as well talk." She was lying in bed, propped up on a pillow, wearing a white hospital gown.

J pulled up the room's one chair and sat down by her bedside.

"I have things to do," Ferguson said apologetically. "If you need me, there's a button . . . " He backed out, bowing slightly, and closed the door.

When he was gone, Zoe said, "I don't like that man. He thinks all you have to do is take a pill and everything will be all right."

"A common superstition of his profession," J replied smoothly.

"Tell me about the fire. Were there many casualties?"

"Twenty-seven dead, by the latest count. I don't remember how many were hurt."

"Twenty-seven dead." She lay back and closed her eyes.

"I think I must be a very selfish woman. That number doesn't seem to mean anything to me."

"No more selfish than the rest of us, Mrs. Smythe-Evans, though perhaps a bit more honest."

"I don't think about all those poor people who got burned up. I don't even think very much about my husband, though he was a good man. I know to some he was a clown, a figure of fun, but he was kind most of the time, and trustworthy and reliable. Reliability is a vastly underrated virtue, I've come to believe. It's like a good English suit; a man can wear it for a long time and it still looks well on him. Yet, though I've honestly tried, I can't seem to burst into hysterical tears over Reginald. Is there something wrong with me?"

"No."

"I'm going to shock you yet. My children. Mrs. Kelly. Are they among the twenty-seven?"

J hesitated, then nodded. "Yes, Mrs. Smythe-Evans."

"You're sure?"

"They were . . . rather badly burned, but my men were able to identify them . . . by their teeth. Your family dentist came down from Norwich with their X-rays. He was very helpful." J was choosing his words with care.

"You see how selfish I am? I don't even think about them, poor lads." Her voice began to quaver and she paused before going on. "Except for Dickie. Dickie wasn't like the others."

J thought she was indeed going to burst into tears, but she gave herself a little shake and opened her eyes. "You see? Selfish to the core! Reginald often accused me of that, of thinking only of myself, of loving only myself. It's a pity he can't be here to enjoy being right again, as he usually was."

J said gently, "To be, as you put it, selfish may be an advantage in a situation like this. You can look at things calmly, plan for the future."

"Future? What future?" she demanded. "I have no future."

"It may not appear so, but . . . "

"I haven't worked at a regular job since my marriage. I have, unfortunately, been a completely faithful wife and mother, and so haven't got a lover waiting in the wings to spirit me away to a new and better life. Oh, I'm sure I won't starve. There will still be plenty of money in the Smythe-Evans coffers, even after inheritance taxes. But a future? That's too grand a word to describe the years I'll be spending in that ugly house in Norwich, listening to echoes and washing dishes for myself, discreetly and with dignity turning into a hag."

"Surely it's not as bad as all that."

"No?" She sat upright and glared at him. "Can you think of anyone on God's green earth who would offer decent employment to a woman of my age and inexperience?"

"Yes I can."

"Who?" Her tone was almost contemptuous.

"Me, Mrs. Smythe-Evans, on behalf of Her Majesty's Special Services, Department MI6A."

"You've finally taken leave of your senses, my dear J," Lord Leighton said, more amused than angry.

Dr. Ferguson, not so good-humoredly, agreed. "That's a layman's diagnosis, but I cannot help but concur."

J, Leighton and Ferguson were in what remained of Ferguson's office. Ferguson sat behind his desk, J sat near the gaping hole in the wall, and Leighton sat near the badly dented filing cabinet, which had been returned to its place against the back of the room. The cabinet was so bent that J suspected it could not be opened without a crowbar.

Leighton continued with agitation, "Of all of us, you've always been the most sticky about security clearances and all that rot, but now . . . "

J smiled. "Mrs. Smythe-Evans is no security risk. I'm certain of that. You see, many years ago I took the liberty of starting a security check on the lady when it appeared that Blade might marry her. He would have had to violate the Official Secrets Act to do it, of course, but he was a hot-blooded lad in those days, if you'll recall. He broke off with her before the investigation was complete, but we've kept track of her ever since. She has never in her life joined any of the wrong organizations, signed any of the wrong petitions, or had any of the wrong friends. Moreover, if she was an agent, even a sleeper under deep cover, we would find her somewhere closer to the seats of power, not married to a C.P.A. in a place like Norwich. I've reactivated her security check, and we should have an official clearance within a fortnight."

Ferguson said stiffly, "Wait until then to swear her in."

J chuckled. "It seems you were not listening, Ferguson old boy. I said I've already sworn her in."

"You can revoke . . . " began the little fat man.

"I've made up my mind, gentlemen. I revoke nothing. If

she doesn't work out, I take full responsibility. Really, since the Katerina Shumilova affair I've become more than somewhat skeptical about the effectiveness of our security precautions. We would probably get a higher percentage of loyal, patriotic Britons if we chucked the whole bloody screening process and recruited our people by lottery from the local Salvation Army breadline." J took out his omnipresent pipe and began filling it with an air of satisfaction.

Lord Leighton said gloomily, "What's done is done, I suppose, but I can't see the good of it."

J answered, tamping down his tobacco, "The simple truth is that we need her. She was able to get a reaction out of Richard . . . "

"A violent reaction," put in Ferguson.

"But a reaction nonetheless," J said. "As things stand, literally everything depends on Richard Blade's recovery." He paused to let this sink in. "Therefore I think we must work closely with her, hiding nothing from her, granting her an unlimited need-to-know. How could we do that if she wasn't one of us, eh?" He lit up, exhaling little puffs of blue-white smoke. The air was filled with the strong but not unpleasant aroma of crude sailor's roughcut tobacco.

"I see there's no arguing with you," Ferguson sighed. "I'll simply have to get used to a strange woman wandering about, without training or aptitude, meddling here, meddling there, asking all manner of absurd questions."

"Not at all, not at all," J assured him. "Mrs. Smythe-Evans will be leaving your domain tonight. So will I."

"But your friend Blade . . . " said Ferguson, surprised.

"Richard Blade will be going with us," J said quietly.

"See here, I . . . " Ferguson sputtered. "My patient . . . "

"Your patient must be removed from the neighborhood of the KALI computer," J said. "Surely you see that. From what little we know about this Ngaa creature, it will probably follow Richard when he leaves, and we must get the Ngaa away from that computer if we hope to prevent it recharging itself at intervals, growing larger and stronger and more dangerous. The Ngaa is no longer a playful nuisance, gentlemen. It has murdered twenty-seven people in a particularly disagreeable fashion. It could kill again at any moment, and we have no defense against it. It could be in this room, listening to every word we say. It could be reading our minds. Yes, I think it likely the creature reads minds. I think it can also project images, make us see things that aren't

71

there. No, doctor, we must snatch Richard Blade away from here, far away. Even Scotland may be too close."

"I gather I am being taken off the case," Ferguson said with ill-concealed resentment.

"At least for the time being," J replied.

"And who will take my place?"

J said thoughtfully, "There is only one other man at all familiar with the ways of the Ngaa. Dr. Saxton Colby."

Ferguson sniffed. "Colby? I understood he'd been drummed out of the corps for conduct unbecoming to a savior."

Lord Leighton chuckled, but J said, "Quite so, old chap, but all the same he's the man we need. He's had more experience with the Ngaa than any of us, and he's had time to think about it. I daresay he's come to some interesting conclusions."

Lord Leighton put in, "Hmm, whatever happened to old Colby? Where did he go?"

"I've made an educated guess, as it were," J answered, then he pointed to the telephone on Ferguson's desk with his pipestem. "If I'm right, that phone should ring any time now."

"What nonsense," Ferguson snorted. "That phone won't . . . "

The phone rang.

Ferguson snatched it up. "Dr. Ferguson speaking! You want to talk to J?"

He handed over the receiver, muttering softly.

"This is J speaking. You remember me?"

A familiar voice sounded in J's ear, somewhat distorted but clearly recognizable. "Of course I do, sir. Did you have your agents track me down?"

"No, I didn't, Dr. Colby," said J, amused. "Ma Bell—as the Americans call her—found you for me. I thought you'd moved to Berkeley, California because of your daughter, you see. I had our telephone operator call Berkeley information, and there was your name, no doubt, in the Berkeley telephone book."

Colby had a deep, well-modulated voice that his patients must have found soothing. "So you know about my daughter?"

"Dr. MacMurdo told me the whole story."

"Then you're probably doubly glad to be rid of me, knowing I'm not only depraved but a raving lunatic." Beneath

Colby's bantering was an undertone of deep, long-nurtured resentment.

"Not at all, doctor. In fact, as far as I'm concerned, you're completely vindicated."

There was a long silence, then Colby said, "Isn't it a bit late? I've built up a new life for myself here. I couldn't come back to England and work for you again even if I wanted to, and I'm not sure I do. I don't mean to sound ungrateful, sir, but . . . " He broke off. He had sounded ungrateful indeed. J thought, *I can't blame him, of course. I would have felt the same way.* When Colby continued, it was with a new tone, a tone of suspicion and a dawning apprehension. "This long distance call must be costing you a pretty penny, sir. Perhaps you'd better come to the point. Why did you phone me?"

"I've seen your daughter."

"Jane?"

"Yes."

"In London?"

"Yes."

"My daughter is dead, sir. She died a long time ago, here in Berkeley." The apprehension was open now, a genuine fear.

"I know. Nevertheless I saw her."

"I've studied this matter for many years, sir. Once I thought, as you do, that I saw her, but now I've become convinced that what I thought was her was something else, something pretending to be her, not a ghost, but something far more dangerous."

"I quite agree," J said.

Suddenly, impulsively, Dr. Colby burst out, "I've changed my mind. I am coming to London. I *must* come!"

"That will not be necessary, Doctor Colby. We would like to come to you, bringing—ah—Jane with us. We will need a room for—er—someone, a room with a lock on the door and, if possible, a fence around the building."

"I understand perfectly. As it happens, sir, I am still plying my trade. I have a small private sanitarium here in the Berkeley hills, in an old mansion that once functioned as an exclusive ballet school. We have locks on the doors and a high wire-mesh fence. No one has ever left without my permission."

"Excellent. We'll hop a jet and see you in a few hours."

"I'll meet you at the airport."

"That will be most kind of you, doctor. And could you bring an ambulance with facilities for restraining an—er—unruly patient?"

"We have such a vehicle."

"I'll have Copra House phone you our ETA. Goodbye, Colby, and thank you for forgiving us."

A moment later J was on the line to Copra House, arranging for the flight.

This done, he turned to Ferguson and said, "I want Richard Blade unconscious until we are in the air, and I mean out cold. Do you understand? If he got rough on the way to the airport, I'm not certain we could handle him."

The fat man nodded. "He can sleep his way across the Atlantic, if you wish."

"Make that all the way to California, if you can do it without harming him," said J.

"He'll be all right." Ferguson lurched to his feet and waddled toward the door. "Do you want some tranquilizer for Mrs. Smythe-Evans?"

J stood up with a grunt. "Zoe doesn't like drugs."

Ferguson paused in the doorway to pass a wink to Lord Leighton. "Well, well," chortled the psychiatrist. "So it's Zoe already, is it? The old rascal hasn't wasted much time getting on a first-name basis, has he?"

After accepting the bribe, the burly orderly continued to hover around behind her with a worried frown on his face.

"I'll be all right," Zoe assured him. "If anything happens I'll call for you."

Reluctantly the orderly went out into the hall and left her alone with Richard.

She approached the foot of the bed, barefoot, clad in a hospital gown, with her purse clutched in her hands.

Richard was asleep, breathing gently, lying on his side. He was free to toss and turn if he wanted to; the orderly had told her Ferguson had ordered the restraining straps removed. They were useless against Blade's appalling strength. All the orderlies and nurses were now armed with tranquilizer pistols. Drugs, it seemed, were the only things that could stop Blade when one of the fits came on.

She halted, gazing uncertainly across the expanse of rumpled blankets at the half-hidden, square-cut face she knew so well. She had watched him sleep many times, long ago.

As she looked at him, year after year fell away into un-

74

reality. She had had a husband. Or had she? She had had children. Or had she? She had had—and still had—a home, a comfortable if tasteless cottage in a small English town. Even that had become vague in her mind, dreamlike. Does one remember what one does while sitting in a waiting room? Does one remember the things one does to kill time?

"Richard," she said softly.

He did not stir.

She moved to his bedside and stood looking down at him. How many mornings had she stood like this in the quiet cottage in Dorset, listening to the distant booming of the sea? How many times had they played the poetry game, one of them quoting a line from a famous poem, then the other trying to quote another line from the same poem?

She thought of Matthew Arnold's "Dover Beach."

"Dick?" she called gently.

He slept on.

She closed her eyes, trying to remember the poem exactly, word for word. Over the years it came back to her. She began, "The sea is calm tonight . . . " Damn! How did the next line go?

"The tide is full, the moon lies fair upon the straits," said Richard Blade.

With a startled cry she leaped back, opening her eyes, almost dropping her purse.

Richard was looking up at her, his dark eyes serious but sane. "Good morning, darling," he said in that cheerful well-spoken light baritone of his.

"Are you . . . are you all right?" she asked fearfully.

"Of course I'm all right. I had a damnable nightmare, that's all. It was one of those bloody awful things that runs on and on, one disaster after another. It seems you married some silly accountant, and there was a machine in it that kept sending me into one hell after another." He raised himself on his elbow and smiled. "No use talking about it. Nothing like that could really happen. Could it, Zoe?"

"No, no, nothing like that could happen."

Blade looked around, frowning with puzzlement. "Where am I? Is this some sort of hospital?"

"Yes. You've . . . you've had an accident." Impulsively she stepped toward him and patted his head.

"What kind of accident?" he demanded.

She tried to think of something plausible, but her mind had gone blank.

"Wait! I think I remember." His powerful fingers closed on her wrist. "A blue cloud. Fire. Pain. Oh my God, the Ngaa! The Ngaa!" His voice rose to a scream. "Oh my God, it's getting into my head!"

"Let me go, Dick." His grip tightened painfully. "Please. Please!"

He did not let go, but screamed wordlessly, thrashing from side to side, his face contorted into a mask of terror, pulling her off her balance. She fell on top of him, sprawling and struggling. "Help!" she screamed. "Help me someone!"

Abruptly he released her and fell back on his pillow, eyes open but blank, face expressionless. She staggered away, half-blinded by her own sudden tears.

"Dick?" she called.

He did not answer, or show in any way that he heard her.

The door burst open and the burly orderly rushed in, tranquilizer gun in hand.

"Is he havin' another of his fits?" the man asked, taking aim.

"Don't shoot him. He's quiet now." She groped her way into the hall.

Dimly she saw J, Lord Leighton and Dr. Ferguson coming toward her on the run. She threw herself into J's arms.

"What's going on here?" asked J.

"He spoke to me," she sobbed.

"Blade? He spoke to you?" J was astonished.

"He sounded perfectly normal, except that he thought he was back in the time when he and I . . . " She could not go on.

"What did he say?" Dr. Ferguson broke in.

"He recited a line of poetry, the same line I heard in my hotel room, the night of . . . the night of the fire." She was thinking, was it Richard Blade who'd spoken to her just now, or was it *someone else?*

76

Chapter 8

Dr. Ferguson waved goodbye with an absurd enthusiasm, standing in front of the hangar in his black plastic raincoat. Lord Leighton, similarly clad, merely hunched his shoulders and glowered like a moody troll. The handshaking and well-wishing was over, and the little scientist was probably already back with his beloved KALI, in mind if not in body.

Then the plane swung around and Ferguson and Leighton were lost to view, though J continued to stare out the port-hole-like window into the night. There was nothing to see but an occasional moving point of light as they taxied swiftly but smoothly out onto the field, but J, lost in thought, did not care.

J had been to the United States before, but not since the Fifties, when he and Richard Blade had tracked a defecting agent from New York to San Francisco in cooperation with the CIA, finally catching up with and killing the fellow in a gay bar in the North Beach district.

J smiled, thinking of the CIA euphemism that had appeared in their report on the action. "The operative was terminated with extreme prejudice." The Yanks were never squeamish about killing, but they were downright Victorian when it came to talking about it.

Some of the CIA men J and Blade had worked with were probably still posted to San Francisco, but J made a mental note not to visit these "old friends." He did not like the CIA, an organization more or less blueprinted by Kim Philby, a British agent who had turned out to be a Russian spy. In J's eyes the CIA still bore the triple mark of its birth: it was as ruthless and power hungry as the worst Russian communist, as stuffy and bureacratic as the worst Englishman, and, most annoying of all, as crass and businesslike as the worst Yank, with its network of secretly owned businesses, which included airlines, hotel chains, laboratories, munitions factories and even a few publishing companies in New York.

J had heard the rumors to the effect that the CIA had assassinated the Kennedy brothers to prevent an investigation of the agency's worldwide billion-dollar clandestine business operations. The general public had laughed at the idea. but J, who knew the CIA better, had not laughed at all. *No*, J concluded, *the less I see of the CIA, the better*.

The plane reached the end of the runway, wheeled about, tested its mighty jet engines, then, after a pause, hurtled down the gleaming wet pavement and was airborne.

J took out his tobacco pouch and began filling his pipe, though the sign above the cockpit door still glowed "No Smoking" as well as "Fasten your seat belts." The plane banked steeply, and J could see, out of the corner of his eye, the pattern of landing lights spread out far below, rendered indistinct by a curtain of mist, then London came into view, glimmering like a heap of red coals spilled out over a vast black hearth.

J tamped down his tobacco.

The plane entered a cloud and London vanished. Drops of moving water appeared on the outer face of the window.

J took out his lighter.

"Do you mind if I smoke?"

Zoe, strapped into the seat next to him, glanced at the still glowing "No Smoking" sign, then shrugged. "Go ahead."

The aroma of sailor's roughcut drifted on the air.

J tilted his seat back to be more comfortable, toying with the idea of going to sleep. He glanced at Zoe. She too had tilted back her seat and her eyes were closed. The lighting was dim.

Richard Blade, he knew, was asleep, strapped into a bunk at the rear of the cabin, under heavy sedation. With Blade was a male nurse and two muscular MI6 men armed with tranquilizer pistols: there were no other passengers on board. Up front rode the crew of three; pilot, copilot and navigator. Though the craft bore the insignia of the Royal Air Force, everyone in it was a member of the Special Branch.

The door under the "No Smoking" sign opened and a tall man in a brown jumpsuit emerged and made his way back along the aisle between the unoccupied seats. It was Captain Ralston, the pilot. When he came to J, he leaned over Zoe and said softly, "Could you come up to the cockpit for a moment, sir?"

J searched the man's impassive face for some clue as to

what might be wrong, but there was nothing there. "Certainly, Captain," J said, unbuckling his seat belt.

"Trouble?" Zoe asked, her eyes fluttering open.

"Nothing serious, madam," Ralston said.

J climbed over her feet into the aisle with a muttered apology and followed Captain Ralston forward. The cockpit, when they entered it, was lit only by the many-colored lights on the control panel and navigation console. The navigator turned in his seat and said, "Good evening, sir." He was a slender, dapper fellow with a neat Vandyke beard. His name was Bob Hall.

"Good evening, Bob," J answered. "What's up?"

Bob hunched over his navigation table, his worried face green in the light from his radar screen. He gestured toward the screen. "A bit of a puzzle, sir. A blip on the radar. Something's following us."

J checked the scope. It was true.

Captain Ralston said, "The control tower picked it up, too, and warned us about it, so it can't be a fault in our equipment."

"How far away is it?" J asked.

"About two kilometers and closing," said Bob Hall. "It's fast, whatever it is, but it seems to be, as far as we can tell, smaller than most aircraft."

The copilot, Floyd Salas, a small dark wiry man, said, "It could be a ground-to-air homing missile."

"There's a cheerful thought," Hall said. "Trust Salas to look on the bright side."

"I don't think it's a missile," J said. He sucked on his pipe, but found it had gone out.

"Should we turn back, sir?" Captain Ralston asked.

"No. That's what the Thing is hoping we'll do," J replied.

"The Thing, sir?" the captain said, raising an eyebrow.

"Is there any way we can get a look at it? Direct visual contact?" J asked.

"Not as long as we stay in this overcast," Ralston answered, glancing at the cockpit windows where nothing was visible but their own darkened and distorted reflections.

"Take her upstairs then," J commanded.

Captain Ralston sat down in the pilot's seat and strapped in. J strapped down in a jump seat directly behind him.

Bob Hall informed the control tower of their plans and got a clearance.

79

The plane began to climb steeply.

Ralston glanced at the altimeter and said, "We should break through any second."

They waited.

Hall said, "The blip's still on the radar. I think . . . yes, the Thing has changed course to follow us up. It's gaining on us. One and a half kilometers and closing."

"What did I tell you?" Salas said gloomily. "It's a homing missile."

No one answered him. The only sound was the rushing muffled roar of the jets.

"One and a quarter kilometers and closing," said Bob Hall crisply, then added with a slight quaver in his voice, "The static is getting bad. I can't understand the control tower."

J muttered, "The Thing seems to have the ability to jam radio transmissions."

Hall reported: "One kilometer . . . I think."

"What do you mean you think?" The Captain glanced back at him, scowling. "You're supposed to know."

"Sorry, sir." Hall was staring at the scope in frustration. "The radar is malfunctioning, too."

J noted that a flock of blips had appeared on the screen, like fireflies, forming no consistent pattern.

At that instant the plane broke out of the cloud cover and soared up into the clear thin air of the lower stratosphere. The moon was full, the stars brighter and more numerous than they could ever be to the earthbound Londoners. The upper surface of the overcast spread out on all sides to the horizon like a vast white undulating desert.

J pressed his face against the window, trying to look back and down.

Hall said, "I don't think you'll be able to see the thing. "It'll come up behind us, in our blind spot."

"Bank then," J said. "I want to get a look at it."

Captain Ralston looked worried. "If we bank, we'll lose air speed."

J snapped, "I don't care. We can't seem to outrun the damn thing anyway. It'll catch up a little sooner, that's all. Bank, Ralston!"

Ralston obeyed.

The area of clouds they had just left came into view. It had a pale red glow to it, but that was the glow of London. There were other areas of muted light across the face of the clouds, each indicating the location of some well-lit city. J knew them; he could have identified each of those cities by the shape and brightness of its glow. He was looking for something else.

And there it was!

A swift-moving sphere of bright blue-white flame burst from the overcast and rose toward him. The color was the same as he'd seen seeping from the seams of KALI's case the night of Richard Blade's return, but much brighter. The Ngaa—for this must be the Ngaa—seemed to fairly seethe and sizzle with energy.

"Beautiful," J whispered in awe.

The Ngaa *was* beautiful as a fallen star.

As the plane leveled out, the Ngaa swung out of sight in the blind spot.

"Have you ever seen anything like that before? demanded Salas in amazement.

J nodded slowly. "Yes, during the war."

Though there had been many wars since, all understood he meant World War II.

"You saw something like that in the war?" Captain Ralston was incredulous.

"Yes," J said thoughtfully. "I was in an RAF bomber over Germany, about to parachute behind enemy lines. I'd heard about them from the Air Force lads, but I didn't believe in them, thought they were airborne folktales, like the gremlins. They often followed Allied bomber squadrons on their missions over the Axis nations, and the flyboys called them Foo Fighters. Yes, that night I saw one just like this, only smaller and dimmer." He was thinking, *There were men under heavy mental stress on those missions. Can mental or emotional stress awaken the same slumbering powers that KALI can?*

Hall, watching his radar screen, broke in, "Your Foo Fighter, if that's what it is, gives off radio waves on the radar wavelengths, and from the way they register, I'd say old Foo is some sort of electromagnetic field, not anything solid. And he seems to be about ten or fifteen times larger than he looks. The outer part of him is visible, nothing but pure energy, and outside the visible spectrum, in the ultraviolet and infrared and beyond. I'm just guessing, though. The damn radar is going crazy! I can't tell anymore, even approximately, how far away he is or where he's located in relation to us."

"Is the radar getting worse?" J demanded.

"By the second!" Hall answered fervently.

"Then I'd say Foo is getting close," said J. "We may already be within his outer edge."

"Here he is!" Salas the copilot cried out.

The wing on his side had become illuminated by flickering blue light and now, as all turned to look, the bright ball of blue-white fire came alongside, not more than a few hundred meters away, drifting with a languid slowness that belied the fact that it was traveling well into supersonic speeds. The instruments on the control panels were registering rapidly changing impossibilities, and J noticed the hairs on the back of his hand standing up and swaying as they had done only once before, on the night of Blade's last return from the X dimensions.

As if racing the hopelessly inferior aircraft, the Ngaa pulled into the lead, passing them with frustrating ease, then rapidly outdistancing them. The instruments resumed some semblance of normality. The hairs on J's wrist stopped swaying.

Captain Ralston sighed with relief. "He's going to leave us alone."

The Ngaa slowed.

"Oh, oh," murmured Ralston.

The Ngaa wheeled in a gleaming arc and came rushing toward them, accelerating.

Salas shouted, "He's going to ram us!"

"Hang on!" warned Ralston, throwing the big jet transport into a steep shearing turn, veering away from the impending collision. The Ngaa shot past in a bright blur.

Salas was muttering something in Spanish, perhaps a prayer. Ralston's anguished voice rang out. "What's that damn fireball doing, anyway?"

J said grimly, "Mr. Foo is trying to communicate with us, in his own quaint way. I believe he is trying to persuade us to turn around and go home."

"What Mr. Foo wants, Mr. Foo gets," Ralston said with feeling, hand closing on the master throttle lever between his seat and Salas's.

J touched the pilot's elbow. "No. Wait. We can beat Mr. Foo."

"Are you insane?" howled Salas. "If that fireball hits the fuel tanks in this plane, we'll go off like a bomb."

"Mr. Foo won't do that," J said firmly. "We have Richard Blade on board, and Mr. Foo needs Richard Blade."

The Ngaa had swung into sight up ahead as they spoke. "Here he comes again," groaned Ralston.

J commanded, "This time don't veer away. If he wants to ram us, let him."

Ralston hesitated a moment, then sighed, "Aye, sir."

Salas whispered, "*Madre* . . . "

The Ngaa was on a collision course, accelerating, blindingly bright like a welding torch. J braced himself for the impact. Ralston sat frozen, gripping the wheel with white fingers.

The cockpit filled with shimmering blue-white light and then . . . *the Ngaa passed through them!*

There was no impact, but J was somehow aware of a rushing movement in the brightness, as of an unseen, unheard, unfelt wind, a hurricane of nothingness, and in the midst of the nothingness was a consciousness, a mind that was ancient beyond belief and intelligent in ways so different from man that words like superior and inferior lost all meaning. And J felt, for an instant, a rush of nameless emotions no man had ever felt before and stayed sane. And J glimpsed, as if in a memory of a nightmare, a city that was made of living matter, that hung, breathing, in a violet sky beneath a glowering red sun, above a planet burnt clean of the last trace of vegetation. And J knew, because the Ngaa knew, that someday soon that great red sun would explode.

Then, inexplicably, the Ngaa was gone.

J sat blinking, his head aching, his eyes watering, numb and uncomprehending. Captain Ralston continued to hold the wheel, pale, eyes glazed. Salas leaned back, eyes closed. Bob Hall sat at his navigator's table, swaying, mouth hanging open. The jet droned on. The full moon stared in at them impassively.

At last J whispered, "Are you all right?"

The others nodded, apparently unable to speak.

"Where did it go?" J asked, beginning to find his voice.

"I don't know," Ralston said, as slowly as if he were relearning the English language, rediscovering the meanings of the simplest words.

They searched the heavens, but the Ngaa was nowhere to be seen.

"Thank God," Bob Hall murmured.

Suddenly the cockpit door burst open with a crash and Zoe stood there, dark hair disheveled, wide-set eyes wild. "Richard . . . " she cried. "He's broken free!"

83

J bgan unsnapping his seat belt. "What about his nurse? His two guards?"

She staggered into the narrow cockpit. "He's killed them!"

J stood up and looked through the doorway. Richard, clad only in a hospital gown, was advancing slowly up the aisle, steadying himself by gripping the backs of the seats. Though the light was dim, there was no mistaking the dark wet bloodstains on his gown.

I'm unarmed, J thought, as a vision of his old Webley service revolver hanging in its holster in the closet of his office flashed through his mind. *Perhaps it's just as well. Wouldn't want to hurt Richard.* J was afraid, but not that afraid.

Ralston's voice was low, guarded. "Shall I flip the plane over on its back, sir. That should . . . "

J answered softly, "No, not yet." He stepped through the doorway, outwardly calm. "Richard! What are you up to now, you young scamp?"

Richard halted a few paces away, a puzzled frown on his face. The expression changed, became alien and opaque, then changed back again. J recieved an unmistakable impression of two separate personalities struggling for control of Blade's features.

"Richard," J called again. "You know me. It's J."

"J?" Blade closed his eyes, swayed, and almost fell.

J advanced a step. "You remember me. I know you do. Come along now, no more of this nonsense." J watched uneasily as Richard's fingers curled into fists. Richard could easily kill a man with one blow of his fist, and J knew it. Killing had always been a routine part of the work of the Special Branch.

J became aware of a curious blue glow in the cabin, a pulsing, shimmering light that was brightest around Richard Blade, but moved over every surface, sometimes so dark a blue as to be all but invisible, sometimes so light as to be nearly white. It was a breathtaking display, like aurora in a polar sky, like reflections in a sea grotto. Here and there a tiny spark arced between two neighboring metal objects, and the bracing smell of ozone was strong. J thought, *The Ngaa is here.*

Barely audible above the drone of the jets was an irregular crackly hiss, and as he listened, J fancied he could hear voices in the hiss, as of a multitude of whisperers. What they were saying J could not quite make out, though the whispers grew steadily louder.

Richard shuffled forward, then halted. The aircraft shifted in its course and the bright moonlight fell on his face like a searchlight. Richard closed his eyes and turned away from the brightness, his features half in light, half in shadow, beads of sweat clearly visible on his forehead. Richard was struggling, J saw, harder than ever before, harder than he had ever had to struggle against enemies who were outside him, not inside.

J said, "Get a grip on yourself, Richard. You can do it."

Richard spoke. J leaned forward to catch the slurred, muttered words. "Yes. I think I can. The Ngaa is strong, so strong."

"But you are stronger."

"But I am stronger. Yes. Yes."

Richard's eyes opened, and it was Richard who looked out through them.

J whispered, "A little more, Richard. Fight him a little more."

"Yes. Yes!"

Abruptly, from everywhere and nowhere came a toneless scream. J heard it not with his ears, but with his mind. Then there was a swirl of glowing fog, a play of cold white flame along the edges of every object in the passenger compartment, then a sensation of dizzy speed as the fog flowed in a rush up through the roof, passing through solid steel as if nothing were there.

From the cockpit Bob Hall called, "The thing's on the radar again, following us, but it seems to be falling back."

Richard stumbled to one side, and fell into a seat where he sat, head in hands, sucking in deep gasping breaths.

J leaned over him, saying, "Are you all right, Richard?"

Blade answered, "Not really. I'm awfully weak. Good Lord, sir, do you know I almost killed you? The Ngaa was forcing me, but I saw it was you, and I fought it."

"Had you tried to fight it before?"

"Yes, but not successfully." Richard's voice was stronger. "Perhaps I needed . . . more motivation. To tell the truth, I'd begun to believe the thing was omnipotent."

"It may attack you again."

"Yes, but I'll know I can beat it, and that should make all the difference."

"I hope so. I certainly hope so." J was not one for physical demonstrations of emotion, but he placed his hand on Richard's shoulder.

Captain Ralston called, "What now, sir?"

J answered, "Set a course for the USA. We proceed as planned."

Richard tried to stand, but fell back into his seat. "I'd like to stay up and chat but . . . "

J said, "You'd better get back in your bunk."

Zoe gently pushed past J's elbow, saying, "Here now, Dick. Let me help you." She did not quite succeed in keeping her voice steady and impersonal.

Chapter 9

"May I smoke, Dr. Colby?"

"By all means, sir."

J lit his pipe and thoughtfully puffed it into life, staring out the tall window over the green garden city of Berkeley to the sailboat-dotted bay and the Golden Gate Bridge beyond. The afternoon sun was bright in an almost cloudless sky that seemed after the gray overcasts of London, unnaturally blue.

J began, "You've examined him?"

"Yes."

"What do you think?"

"The prognosis is favorable, certainly more favorable than it was in the case of poor Dexter. Your Richard Blade would seem to be perfectly normal except for one thing."

"What's that?"

"He's living in the past, or to be more exact, he appears to have lost a span of ten years or more."

"Lost?"

"Forgotten. Repressed. In his own mind he is a much younger man than he really is, a man who has never visited the X dimensions, full of the confidence of his training and his successful career in British intelligence. He is a man in love with and engaged to a Zoe Cornwall, a Zoe Cornwall who was never married to Reginald Smythe-Evans, never lost her children, never was widowed."

J turned to face the man. "But Dr. Colby, he seemed to remember everything on the plane, even the Ngaa."

"He remembers nothing of what happened on the plane. After all, he killed three of his own organization's men with his bare hands. That can't be an easy thing to face. And the Ngaa is what drove him into amnesia in the first place. At present Ngaa is no more to him than a meaningless word."

J stood, back to the window, studying the psychiatrist, thinking, *Can I trust the judgment of this fellow?*

Had he not devoted himself to psychology, Dr. Saxton Colby could have been a actor. He had an actor's deep, carrying voice, an actor's high cheekbones and expressive lean face, an actor's lithe and graceful body, an actor's shock of long disheveled iron-gray hair. J knew, from a cursory study of Colby's dossier at Copra House, that he had been raised in a theatrical family, and that his father had been a famous Shakespearean performer.

J had known actors, including a few of the more famous film stars. They were a self-centered lot at best, yet here was a man who had broken with that world to devote himself to studying and helping others. *Yes, I think I can trust him.*

Colby leaned back in his leather-upholstered swivel chair, looking up at J calmly, confidently, slacks-clad long legs crossed, white short-sleeved sport shirt open at the throat. "One progresses, as they say, two steps forward and one step back," he said.

J began to pace the room, puffing moodily. "If only we had more to go on."

"It would be easier," Dr. Colby agreed. "At first glance Dexter and Blade would appear to be the only recorded cases of this particular syndrome."

J halted in midstride. "What do you mean, 'At first glance?' "

Colby had swiveled to follow J's movements across the large room. "You are familiar with the work of the American student of the unusual, Charles Fort?"

"Yes, as a matter of fact. I've read his book *Wild Talents,* and couldn't help but notice the similarity between his 'Fortean Events' and the things that the Ngaa has been doing."

"Then you understand the implications. The Ngaa has invaded our universe many times in the past and may continue in the future. I've studied the Ngaa. I think I've studied this being more than any other living man, and in my studies I've found that others have gone before me, attempting to uncover the true nature of the creature, if one can call it a creature. Charles Fort was not the only one, by any means. Some of them have, I think, come much closer than he did."

"Who, for example?"

Colby searched through the piles of papers and books on his desk and came up with a sheaf of papers. "I don't know who wrote this pamphlet, but I suspect it was a turn-of-the-century occultist named DeCastries."

J took the copy and examined it. It was perhaps twenty pages long, on eight and a half by eleven sheets. The title caught his eye. "Megapolisomancy." J raised a questioning eyebrow.

"DeCastries had a theory that what we call hauntings or Fortean events were caused by some sort of paramental beings that were attracted by large cities, that somehow fed off the life energies of the masses of people jammed together there. I think he had at least part of the truth. The Ngaa seems to like big cities, but it has been known to function outside them."

"Where did you get this thing?" J was leafing through it, reading a line here, a line there.

"I joined an occultist society called the Rosicrucian Order. Their world headquarters is just south of here, in San Jose. I worked my way up from level to level until I reached the point where they would allow me to read the books they keep in their restricted library, books they won't show the general public or even the novices, though I should tell you the books they do let the novices see are quite amazing. I found a great deal, there in the restricted stacks, but this was so interesting I took the liberty of copying the more relevant passages."

J read aloud, " 'Gargantuan tombs or monstrous vertical coffins of living humanity, a breeding ground for the worst of paramental entities.' Just the sort of hocus-pocus one would expect to find in the library of some lunatic fringe secret society."

"Laugh if you will," Colby said soberly, "but if you look into the matter you'll find that so-called lunatic fringe occultist secret societies have had a hand in every major political upheaval in history. There were Masons in the American Revolution, Rosicrucians in the French Revolution, the Vril Society backing Hitler. There was Rasputin, the Compte de St. Germaine, so many others. Surely you, of all people, are aware that there are things that are not told to the ordinary man in the street."

"Hmm. Yes. You have a point." J sat down across the desk from Colby and began idly fishing around in the pile of books and papers. "All the same, here's something more my style." He picked up a paperback copy of *The Star Rover*, by Jack London.

"Ah yes," Colby said. "London's last major work. As you

may recall, it is about a man who can travel freely through space and time, as freely as our friend Richard Blade."

"What are you trying to tell me?"

"London was a friend of DeCastries, and the center of a literary coterie that included the poet George Sterling and the fiction writers Ambrose Bierce and Clark Ashton Smith, the same coterie that founded, in 1909, the prestigious California Writers Club. There were others in the group whose reputations have been less lasting, who have been unjustly eclipsed by the more famous members. Nora May French, for example. And there was some sort of scandal about the founding of the California Writers Club that all writers on the subject hint at but none explain. DeCastries, Bierce, Smith, London, French, Sterling . . . They knew something, J! They knew something about the X dimensions, and they knew something about the Ngaa."

"What makes you so sure?"

"It runs like an obsessive undercurrent through the work of all them, now hidden, now openly revealed. Ambrose Bierce writes about invisible beings in his 'The Damned Thing,' London takes up the same theme in 'The Shadow and the Flash,' and Smith repeats it in 'The Double Shadow.' And all of them wrote of other worlds, exactly the sort of worlds Richard Blade has so often visited. Have you read 'Poseidonis' by Smith? 'Before Adam' by London? 'Wine of Wizardry' by George Sterling?"

"No, I'm sorry. My reading has been in other areas."

"Read them, my friend! You will see that this little band of writers and poets had somehow learned to catch at least glimpses of what is out there somewhere, in the X dimensions. And you will see that they had met, out there, the Ngaa. In 1973 the Mirage Press published a collection of fragmentary essays and letters of Clark Ashton Smith entitled *Planets and Dimensions*. Here, let me show you." He rummaged through the stack and came up with an unpretentious white-jacketed paperback.

J took the book and read, " 'About 1918 I was in ill health and, during a short visit to San Francisco, was sitting one day in the Bohemian Club, to which I had been given a guest's card of admission. Happening to look up, I saw a frightful demonian face with twisted rootlike eyebrows and oblique fiery-slitted eyes, which seemed to emerge momentarily from the air about nine feet above me and lean toward my seat. The thing disappeared as it approached me, but left an ineffaceable impression of malignity, horror and loathsomeness."

"He saw it," insisted Colby. "He saw it in broad daylight. Clark Ashton Smith saw the Ngaa, as it chose to show itself to him. I have spent my every spare moment since coming to America in places like the Rosicrucian Library, the Bancroft Library of the University of California, the California Room of the Oakland Public Library and Oakland's Jack London Room, at the Jack London Museum in Glen Ellen, where Russ Kingman, the curator, has helped me track down obscure information unknown to all but the most devoted Jack London aficionados. Bit by precious bit, a picture has formed. Yes, bit by bit, like a man reconstructing a dinosaur from a million tiny bones, I have reconstructed the lives of those men and women who, in the early years of the twentieth century, found a route into another world.

"It was all part of what Jack London termed a 'search for a natural explanation for the supernatural.' London, you know, had a mother who was a spirit medium, yet he early fell under the influence of Marxist dialectical materialism. For him, at least, some way of harmonizing the spiritual with the material was a psychological necessity. The others, each in a different way, felt the same need.

"The search was part hobby, part obsession, and it led them into researches into the occult, pursued off and on over most of their adult lives. Together with H.P. Lovecraft, with whom Smith carried on an extensive correspondence, they evolved the theory that there were creatures of some sort trapped in another dimension who had once ruled Earth and sought to return and rule it again, and that attempts by these beings to break through into our world explained all the various strange events usually ascribed to supernatural causes. These writers formed a kind of brotherhood, vowed to secrecy and, if and when any one of them sensed the Ngaa coming for them, to suicide."

I was surprised. "Suicide, Dr. Colby?"

"Yes, suicide. One thing they found out which you may not yet have guessed is that the Ngaa, under certain conditions, has the power to kidnap someone from our dimension and return with him to its own dimension. Against such an abduction, death was their only defense."

"What finally happened to them all?"

"About DeCastries I know almost nothing. He is such an obscure figure he may be a fictional character, invented by the others, or a pen name for someone. Jack London's Wolf House mansion in the wilderness of the Valley of the Moon burst into flames and was totally gutted the night before London was to move into it, and the fire remains unexplained to this day. Not long after, London died, and London buffs are still debating whether it was by natural causes, suicide or murder. Nora May French and George Sterling poisoned themselves. Ambrose Bierce wrote a postcard to a friend from Mexico saying 'Pray for me—real loud,' then vanished without a trace, though the U.S. government searched for him for years."

"What about Clark Ashton Smith?"

"After a brief career as a writer of weird tales, he abandoned literature and became a hermit, spending the rest of his life sculpting horrible yet frightfully lifelike statues of monsters."

Of the mansion's former use as a ballet school, there remained only a few reminders. One of these was the floor to ceiling mirrors in the gymnasium. These mirrors faced each other in such a way that J, when he looked into one of them, seemed to see a line of replicas of himself, a line that stretched in two directions to infinity. It was a vaguely disquieting illusion, but nevertheless it was in the gym that J installed his scrambler phone, on the wall, plugging in to a pre-existing outlet. The room was almost never used during the summer, when the patients could get their exercise out of doors, and California was at this time suffering a kind of out-of-season summer, one of the worst droughts in its history. There were, of course, no telephone outlets in the patients' rooms, and J was now living in one of these rooms.

On his first day at Dr. Saxton Colby's sanitarium, J had telephoned Copra House, "keeping in touch," as he put it. He had phoned again on the second day, the third and the fourth. It was not until the fifth day that he had finally phoned Lord Leighton at the Project. He had reasoned, on a conscious level, that Copra House would inform him if there was any trouble in the underground computer complex, but perhaps on an unconscious level he was afraid of what Leighton might have to tell him, afraid that the Ngaa had not left London but had remained behind to work some new mischief.

"Lord Leighton here."

"This is J, old boy."

"Don't 'old boy' me. You took your bloody time ringing me up. Been too busy sunning yourself at the seaside with those American film stars, I fancy."

"No such luck. Tell me Leighton, how has it been going there?"

"If you mean by that, have I been having trouble with things that go bump in the night, the answer is no. Since you left, everything's been quiet. Quiet as a tomb, you might say. How about at your end?"

"Quiet here, too. We had a bit of trouble with the Ngaa immediately after takeoff, but since then nothing."

"That's good news at any rate."

"I'm not so sure."

"Oh? The Ngaa has picked up its toys and gone home, and now you miss it?"

"No, no, but I'm getting a feeling about how the Ngaa operates. For example, I saw a picture of Dr. Colby's daughter Jane, the one who might have committed suicide."

"And she looked exactly like the little girl you saw from the window of my study?"

"No, she looked completely different. Colby's daughter had black hair in bangs. The girl I saw was a blonde with a pony tail."

"My word! Then who was it that you saw?"

"It was the Jane Colby I had expected to see. MacMurdo never actually described her, so I put together an image in my head of what a girl of that age, living in the states at that time, ought to look like. The Ngaa plucked that image out of my mind and presented it to me as a reality, knowing I'd accept it because it fulfilled my preconceived ideas. You see what I'm driving at?"

"Not really."

"The Ngaa believes in giving people what they want. That's how it ropes people in, you see. That's how it roped in Dr. Colby, by allowing him to believe his daughter had returned to him."

"Does Colby still believe that?"

"No, his researches have convinced him the so-called ghost he saw in Scotland was a pure illusion. He didn't like that conclusion, but he accepted it when the evidence became overwhelming. He's a father, Leighton, but he's also a scientist, and the scientist in him finally won the argument. It was a brutal disillusionment."

93

"A pity, but I still don't see . . ."

"Think, Leighton, think! What do we want most now? To be rid of the Ngaa! So the Ngaa, like a good genie, is granting our wish, but only until we drop our guard. Then I promise you the Ngaa will be back, and with a few surprises we may find decidedly unpleasant."

"Hmm. You may be right. But where will the Ngaa turn up, there where you are or here?"

"Here, I think. Richard is here."

"That should make the Prime Minister happy. His flunkies have been crawling like lice all over the installation, making a bloody nuisance of themselves for the last few days. They're doing an inventory, they say, with an eye toward liquidating our assets. I hope you haven't forgotten the PM's ultimatum. He said he'd shut us down if Richard wasn't normal within two weeks. Eight days of that two weeks are gone already. We've only six days left. Do you think we'll make the deadline?"

J sighed. "I don't know. We're progressing."

"Could Richard give a reasonable imitation of a sane man?"

"So long as nobody asked him anything about the last ten years."

"Not good enough, I'm afraid. But bear in mind that we don't need a real cure, just one real enough to fool the PM and his examiners."

J was about to reply with some angry objection, but instead got a grip on himself and said, "I'll keep that in mind." Leighton was only being his usual pragmatic and brutally frank self.

"Anything more to tell me, old boy?" Leighton added.

"No."

"Then I'll ring off. I'm frightfully busy keeping these idiots from breaking things."

"One question, Leighton. Have you left the settings the same on KALI?"

"Yes. You think we might . . ."

"It's possible." J thought, *It's possible, even though the PM has forbidden it, even though the danger is beyond calculation. It's possible that we may have to send Richard Blade through into the Ngaa's dimension.*

"Don't wait so long to call me again," Leighton said.

"I won't. Goodbye, old chap."

"Goodbye."

J hung up, stepped back from the wall, and inspected his pocketwatch. As he did so, he could have sworn he saw something very odd out of the corner of his eye. He whirled to stare into one of the mirrors.

Had one of his many reflections moved more slowly than the others?

No, of course not. That was impossible.

The setting sun reddened the gray facade—it had once been white—of the sanitarium, a three-story pseudo-Grecian building of ample proportions. The front door opened and Zoe and Richard emerged, blinking and shading their eyes. They crossed the narrow porch, between the fluted Corinthian columns that framed the entrance, and descended the wide marble staircase. At the foot of the steps, on massive rectangular pedestals, two lifesize white stone lions crouched. As she neared one of them, Zoe could not help but notice the poor animal had lost its left ear and the tip of its tail, and was badly cracked across the haunches.

She sighed and thought, *Too bad.*

Richard took her hand. Had he heard her sigh?

They walked along a broad stretch of paving. Weeds grew in the joins between the paving stones, and in the cracks in the stones themselves where the smooth pale surface was broken. She heard soft footsteps behind her but did not look around. She knew two guards were following her, armed with the ever-present air-propelled tranquilizer dart guns.

By the tall flagpole, as thick as a man's arm, they halted. Richard, squinting upward, said, "I don't see the good old Union Jack." There was no flag on the pole at all.

Zoe laughed. "I doubt if anyone has thought of flying it."

Blade was half-serious, half-joking. "This place is a British possession, isn't it? Like an embassy?" He let go of her hand.

"Not really, Dick. And I doubt if Dr. Colby wants to attract attention."

"You're quite right, of course." He bent, grasped the pole and gave it an experimental tug. It remained firm in its base, though it gave a little, very little.

"What on earth are you doing?" she demanded.

"Nothing." He straightened, a thoughtful enigmatic expression on his tanned angular features. There were beads of sweat on his forehead, though the late afternoon air was quite cool. She wondered, *Had he been trying to pull the flagpole up by the roots? Whatever for?* She eyed his power-ful torso. He wore a white short-sleeved T-shirt with his white slacks and tennis shoes. If he wanted to do something that insane, he could probably manage it. He noticed her looking at him and smiled. "Come along, Zoe. Let's explore the grounds of our prison."

He began walking, drawing her along by the hand.

"This is no prison," she protested.

"Then let's leave."

"You know we can't do that, Dick."

"I rest my case, love. It *is* a prison."

"It's a hospital. You're here to get well."

"I'm not sick." He shot her a glance from his dark, glit-tering eyes. "And you're not a nurse."

This was a reference to the white nurse's uniform she was wearing. They had both come from England without clothing, and had been outfitted from the sanitarium's sup-ply of staff uniforms.

He had halted again and was looking through a grove of fragrant eucalyptus and pine trees at where the sun silhou-etted the Golden Gate Bridge. He said, "I can't believe the KGB would build a second Golden Gate Bridge just for me."

"What do you mean by that?"

"I says you're an agent now, so I can tell you everything, can't I?" As he spoke he studied her face.

"Of course."

"The Ruskies have a department called TWIN. They school some of their men there to look, act and think like every one of our important agents, so that, at the right moments, they can send in one of their doubles to replace one of us. They have training towns in Russia, you see. Exact duplicates of places in England and the USA."

"And you thought this was a duplicate Berkeley, some-where in the Soviet Union?" She was awed. This kind of thinking, this professional, matter-of-fact, businesslike para-noia was new to her.

"The idea crossed my mind, love," Blade said lightly. "But even with their budget, the Ruskies wouldn't build any-thing quite so grand. I'm prepared to believe, for the mo-ment at least, that we are where you say we are, and that you are who you say you are."

"Well, thank you for that, anyway!" Zoe was indignant.

Richard began walking again. She ran a few steps to catch up.

"I've always liked Berkeley," he mused. "J and I were here once. Did he tell you? A bit of the wet stuff in cooperation with the yanks. A lot goes on here. A spy can see plenty simply by renting a room in the hills and a telescope." He gestured toward the bay. "When a navy vessel drops anchor out there, it's no use trying to hide the fact."

They came to a wire-mesh fence topped with barbed wire.

Blade said, "Is this electrified?"

"I don't know."

"Probably not. But it doesn't matter."

He started along the fence. She hurried after him. "Dick, what are you doing, anyway?"

"Taking my evening constitutional, love. You say I'm sick. Well, what could be better for me than a brisk walk out in the fresh air?"

She caught up and he encircled her waist with a powerful arm and gave her a peck on the forehead. She felt a rush of emotion that should have died long ago, yet still remained as strong as ever. That painful ambivalence! At one instant she felt warm and protected, at the next vulnerable and afraid, as if Richard were an ancient god who might in one mood perform miracles of healing, and in another mood demand a human sacrifice.

How could she propitiate him?

Her body! That would satisfy him. It had always satisfied him before. How strange it was to love a man, and at the same time fear him! With Reginald it had been perhaps a little dull, but not frightening. At least not frightening!

"Oh, Dick," she whispered, pulling his head down, pulling herself up. They kissed. She realized that if he killed her she wouldn't mind. It would be all right.

The darkness was settling in around them.

A plane passed overhead, blinking its lights red, green, white, red, green, white.

Gently she pulled herself free of his arms.

"Will you come with me to my room?" she asked, her voice shaking.

He nodded, but his face was in shadow so she could not read his expression.

They started back toward the mansion.

Zoe noticed, as she passed them, the two white-clad guards standing in the bushes, tranquilizer pistols in hand.

When Richard emerged from Zoe's room shortly before noon the following day, J and two guards were patiently waiting for him in the hall.

"Good morning, J," Richard said, smiling.

"Good morning, Richard," J answered, returning the smile somewhat stiffly. "You look refreshed."

"I feel positively top-hole." Richard yawned and stretched. Indeed, in his white T-shirt and white slacks (though the slacks were rumpled) he looked top-hole, at least physically.

J said, "You had an appointment with Dr. Colby this morning. Did you forget?"

"That's right!" Blade snapped his fingers. "It completely slipped my mind. I'm awfully sorry, really I am. Why didn't you remind me?"

J looked down, shuffling his feet uncomfortably. "I did not think you'd want to be disturbed."

"You're always a true gentleman, sir. How refreshing in this decadent age!" At times like this Blade was as charming as a pet giant panda. J could not stay angry with him.

"Well, come along to lunch, Richard. Dr. Colby will be able to give you another appointment this afternoon, I'm sure." J turned and started down the hall.

"That's good of him." There was no trace of sarcasm in Richard's voice, yet J glanced at him sharply. Blade's rough-hewn features were expressionless, perhaps too expressionless. J realized with uneasiness that Richard's animal cunning was returning much more rapidly than his memory.

The two men went downstairs side by side in silence, the guards a few steps behind.

As they entered the sunlit dining room, J noticed Richard's glance darting around the room, taking in every detail in an instant. The rectangular tables. The paper plates and plastic tableware. The paper tablecloths. The patients, some of whom turned to eye the newcomers sullenly. The doctors and nurses at the head table. J thought, *What's he looking for?*

Colby waved and smiled.

"Let's sit at the head table," J suggested.

"As you like," Blade agreed.

They made their way down the center aisle, between two rows of tables. The murmur of conversation went on. Some of the patients had begun eating. Others were waiting as the harassed waiters rushed to and fro from the kitchen and back. Too few waiters. J took this as yet another indication, that poor Colby's sanitarium was, at best, a marginal operation from the financial standpoint.

Colby stood up and leaned forward to shake hands, first with Richard, then with J. J noted (and he was sure Richard must have noticed too) that the lean psychiatrist's palms were sweating.

"Do sit down," Colby said brightly. "And where is the charming Mrs. Smythe-Evans?"

"She decided to sleep in," Richard answered, pulling back a chair.

Colby sat down. "I'm sure she'll be able to find a snack later."

"No doubt," Richard agreed.

J and Richard found themselves facing Colby across the table, the patients behind them. With a quick glance over his shoulder, J reassured himself that the two guards were still on duty, then saw that Blade was watching him and felt, for some reason, deeply embarrassed.

Colby too was ill at ease, so it was Blade who, after a considerable period of strained silence, said, "I want to apologize for missing my session with you this morning, Dr. Colby."

Colby, speaking with his mouth full, answered, "That's quite all right."

"Could I have another appointment for this afternoon?" Blade inquired.

J felt a twinge of surprise. This was the first time Richard had shown more than the most perfunctory co-operation in his therapy. Now, suddenly, Richard was requesting an appointment!

Colby, also surprised, said, "Of course. Two o'clock is open."

"Two o'clock it is." Richard smiled warmly, then added, "I've been bonkers for over ten years, haven't I?"

Colby said sharply, "Did someone tell you that?"

Richard shook his head. "If you wanted to keep it a secret, you should have gotten rid of all the calendars in this place."

J said guardedly, "You haven't been—as you put it— bonkers for that long."

"How long then?" Richard demanded.

"A little over a week," J replied.

Colby shot J a warning glance. "It's best if these things come out under controlled conditions, during therapy. Has your memory started to return, Mr. Blade?"

Blade mused, chewing on a chicken leg, then said, "So, it's amnesia I'm in for. No, I'm afraid my memory isn't coming back, but I do have eyes."

Very sharp eyes, thought J. He wondered how long Richard had been playing dumb and watching, watching, watching. In fact, Richard was not above pretending not to remember even though completely recovered. The man was a trained special agent, damnit! Deception was his business. And they had only Richard's few, perhaps deliberately misleading, remarks to go on.

J found himself staring at Blade's profile, trying to read that unreadable face.

Blade said suddenly, "Have I killed someone?"

Colby stiffened but did not reply. J, too, found himself unable to speak.

Blade nodded slowly. "I see that I have."

Colby said, "How did you guess?"

Blade gestured with his plastic fork toward the two nearby guards. "You're watching me so closely. You're all so frightened of me. I knew I must have done something frightful." Who was it I did in?"

Colby said, "It wasn't your fault. It's better we don't talk about it now." He had turned quite pale.

Blade said, "Not polite lunch conversation, eh? Well, I'll see you at two this afternoon, doctor. I promise you a more than usually interesting hour."

Richard was the only one at the table who was smiling.

Chapter 10

Dr. Saxton Colby was radical in his willingness to explore the more hidden and occult aspects of the mind, to advance into those shadowed areas normally reserved for quacks, charlatans, fanatics and madmen. In this he followed the example of the great psychologist C.J. Jung. In his therapeutic methods, however, Colby was an arch-conservative. Thus his office was furnished with an old-fashioned psychoanalytical couch, not unlike the one used by Dr. Freud in Austria in the early years of this century, the favored symbol of cartoonists to this day. The couch was a Victorian antique, armless, raised at one end, deep-tufted, fringed all around, and upholstered in maroon crushed plush. As Richard Blade sat down on it, Colby looked on with ill-concealed agitation.

"Lie back and relax, Richard," the doctor instructed.

Richard obeyed. "Like this?"

"Exactly."

Colby quickly crossed to close the heavy maroon window drapes, plunging the small cluttered room into semidarkness, then returned to seat himself behind the couch on a sturdy Morris chair, outside Richard's field of vision, next to a three-foot-tall pedestal on which rested a lifesize bronze bust of the logotherapist Joseph Fabry.

Colby opened his notepad, and with his faintly gleaming silver ballpoint pen wrote Richard's name and the date at the head of the first blank page he came to. He glanced at Richard, who seemed, in white T-shirt and slacks, almost to be glowing. He thought, *Today we'll make some progress.* Five daily one-hour sessions had thus far yielded Colby little more than Richard's name, rank and serial number, plus the definite impression that Richard had mislaid ten years and was in no hurry to track them down. Colby pursed his lips and waited. When Richard said nothing, he prompted, "In the dining room you promised me an interesting hour."

"So I did," Richard mused. "I fully intend to keep that promise."

"Have any more memories returned?"

"No, but I am gradually beginning to understand what's happened to me, by detective work rather than recall. You're a detective of sorts, aren't you?"

"One might say that."

"Your job is to unearth all your patients' dirty little secrets. That's detective work. You might do well in my line, doctor. I think I'd do well in yours."

"You don't say. Do you think you could—as you put it—unearth all my dirty little secrets?" Colby had confronted this psychological gambit before. In fact, sooner or later every patient took a turn at trying to switch places with the therapist. They were never very good at it, but the false ideas they came up with were often their own problems projected, and thus worth listening to.

"Nothing profound, of course. Your speech tells me you've lived in London, Scotland and Ireland," said Blade.

"Well, not bad. You're right so far."

"You were educated in the USA, or at least went to a university here."

"Right again. Did you get that from the way I talk?"

"No, but from where I'm lying I can see the books on your shelves. All the college-level texts are from American, not British, publishers."

"Bravo!" Colby was genuinely amused.

"The books also tell me you have a lasting and deep interest in the occult. It would take time to collect as many occult titles as you have, and some of them are books of considerable rarity and value. You've spent money on those books, doctor, as well as time."

"Right again!"

"You come from a theatrical family . . ."

"What? How did you guess that?"

"Your movements. The way you project. The theater—probably the legitimate theater—has left its mark on you, yet you yourself have no greasepaint in the blood. Your library, though it contains works of fiction, does not boast a single collection of plays or book on the theater."

"Very clever, Mr. Blade."

"You did not like your father."

"Now you're simply guessing."

"No, I'm not. Your profession is so profoundly different

from his you could not have chosen it without a violent rupture. Show business is a particularly difficult subculture to escape from, but you appear to have managed it all too well. At the same time your occultism and your stance in your profession is rebellious. I sense in your attitude toward the father-figures of psychology a carried-over hostility toward your own father. A substantial hostility, since it still influences you so much after all these years!"

Colby had become uncomfortable. Richard was hitting much too close to the mark. "That's enough Sherlocking, Richard. Can we get back to you? It is you, not I, who has a problem."

"I've solved my problem, doctor."

"You have? How?"

"By forgetting it."

Colby burst out laughing. When he could speak, he said, "I shall remember that one, Richard. You're a wit, aren't you, as well as a detective and amateur psychotherapist?"

"On your desk is a photo of a little girl. From the fading of the color it must be an old photo. Your daughter?"

"Yes, but . . ."

"Odd you have no more recent photos. Is she dead?"

"Yes, only I . . ."

"And no photos of a wife, no photos of the girl's mother."

"Damnit, I . . ."

"Anger? Are you angry? The mother's not dead, yet it is obvious neither she nor any other woman is sharing your present life. If she were dead we'd see her photo alongside your daughter's, wouldn't we? And I've seen how you speak to the female members of the staff, of whom there are surprisingly few. I sense a divorce, Dr. Colby, a divorce in which you were deeply hurt, a divorce from which you have not even now recovered, a divorce that poisons your relationship with every woman you meet."

Colby leaped to his feet. "Stop that! Stop!"

"Am I wrong?" Richard asked mildly.

After a long pause Colby said, "No, you're quite right." His voice was barely audible. "But I am not the patient here. You are."

Blade said gently, "Sit down, Saxton." Colby was about to protest against the undue familiarity, the blatant bossiness, but instead he did as he was told. Blade went on, "I know you want to help me. Believe me when I say you cannot. Each of us has a blind spot. Mine is that I cannot accept the kind of help you offer, even to save my life. I have always made my own decisions, helped myself, and my training has enforced that habit. In the field I have always had to act more or less on my own, and I certainly could never confide in anyone. As J may have told you, I have not been a docile agent, have even deliberately disobeyed orders several times, though thankfully it all turned out right. I have made mistakes, but they have been my own mistakes. I'm rather fond of them, since they've taught me so much. Now, with or without my memory, I intend to continue to make my own decisions, to ask no help from anyone, to reserve for myself all judgments of what is true and false, right or wrong, real or unreal. Do you understand?"

Colby felt a gray hopelessness, which he did not bother to conceal, as he replied, "I understand that there is no point in you and I continuing to work together."

Richard sat up and turned to look at Colby, saying, "That's not so, Saxton. While I am the sort who, ultimately, can't be helped, you are a different breed of man. You care what people think of you, you listen to advice, you can accept help."

"From whom?"

"From me, Saxton."

Saxton considered this for some time, then said softly, "All right."

When the hour reserved for Richard was up, Colby's secretary said over the intercom, "Time for your next patient, doctor." Her tone was crisp and businesslike.

Colby answered, his voice oddly hoarse, "Cancel all my appointments for the rest of the afternoon."

"Yes, sir." The woman was puzzled but submissive.

Four hours later the door to Dr. Colby's office opened and Colby and Richard Blade emerged. Blade had his arm around the doctor's shoulders and the secretary could not help but notice that Colby's eyes were red, as if he'd been crying.

"Is there something wrong, doctor?" she demanded.

"Not anymore," Colby answered, a strange peaceful smile lighting up his gaunt features. She had never seen such relief, such calm, such inner stillness in a human face. It actually frightened her.

The two men passed her and entered the hallway, and she could have sworn she heard Dr. Saxton Colby turn to the hulking Richard Blade and say, "Thank you, Blade. Thank you. Thanks."

She rolled her eyes heavenward, then went on reading her magazine.

After supper, when Zoe and Richard went upstairs, the usual guards trailed along behind them, two husky white-clad men with tranquilizer pistols.

"Do they watch you all the time, Dick?" she asked.

Richard smiled ironically. "When I'm safely locked in my room at night, they are satisfied to only spot-check me at half-hour intervals."

"They lock you in every night?"

He nodded. "That's right. They either lock me in or watch me. I daresay there was someone outside your door all last night." He gestured toward a door they were passing. "They keep their weapons in there. Note the combination padlock. That's a mistake."

"A mistake?"

"On their part." He blew on his fingertips. "Colby is keeping special services men here, and many of us have a way with combination locks. Dr. Colby is a good man in his field, but MI6 is well rid of him. He's too careless."

Blade opened the door to his bedroom and ushered her in. When he had closed the door he stood a moment, finger to lips, then relaxed, saying, "They didn't lock us in. That means they'll be standing guard out there." He crossed to the window. "I should warn you not to say anything obscene. We wouldn't want to shock whoever it is that is on duty at the listening post."

She followed him. "Listening post?" she said.

"Of course. We must assume this room is bugged. And of course the heavy bars on the window are rigged with a burglar alarm. Isn't it reassuring to know we're being taken care of so well?"

She stood beside him at the barred window, watching the color fade from the evening sky. His arm slipped around her shoulders and rested there, and once again she felt that familiar rush of ambivalent emotion he always inspired in her. He was like a bear in a cage, warm, seemingly docile, yet not tame, not a safe pet, perhaps dangerous. Was he plotting his escape? Was escape possible? No, there was no way even Richard Blade could get out of this place!

Abruptly Richard broke in on her thoughts with, "At supper Dr. Colby called you Mrs. Smythe-Evans. Did you

105

marry during those years I've forgotten?" His voice was casual, as if commenting on the weather.

"Yes, but you must understand . . ."

"I was under the impression that you were going to marry me."

"That wasn't possible." She was flustered, a little defiant.

"Why not?" He was calm, seemingly emotionless.

"You were a stranger. Everything about you was a secret. But even so, I was willing. It was you, after your first enthusiasm wore off, who backed away from the idea."

She saw a grimace pass fleetingly across his face, saw his eyes close. He said, "I'm remembering things. More than I've let on. I've been remembering bits and flashes since . . . I don't know. But I've been pushing them out of my mind. They're too insane to be real."

"Remembering what?"

"A machine. Some kind of computer that sends me into alien universes."

"It's not insane, Dick. It's true. That machine is what destroyed our relationship, though I didn't know it at the time."

"It's true? The swordsmen? The primitive societies? The monsters? It's not just my nightmares?"

"It's all true."

"And the Ngaa?" Richard's forehead glistened with sudden sweat. "Is the Ngaa real too?" He stepped away from her, looking at her intently.

She reached out and grasped his hand. "Yes," she said softly. "Do you remember the Ngaa?"

"No. Yes. I think so. I see a city drifting high in a dim red sky . . . a dying sun . . . a flame-blasted planet below . . . a hovering ball of blue-white fire . . . passageways like crystal cathedrals . . . a jumble of dreams. Oh Zoe, suddenly my head is full of images, impossible images! Was I really there? In the home of the Ngaa?"

"Yes, you were! I wish I could tell you the Ngaa is nothing but a dream, but I can't. It's real and dangerous. And it's followed you here. Can you remember that, too?"

He nodded slowly, his face somber in the failing light. "Yes, I remember. I was in an aircraft, over London. The Ngaa attacked me, entered my mind. But I drove it out! By God, I won against it."

She hugged him excitedly. "Oh, Dick, that's right! We must tell J and Dr. Colby!"

But he stopped her as she turned toward the door, holding her shoulders in his powerful fingers, and he said, "Not yet. Let me work on my memories alone for a while. If I'm disturbed they may slip away." She wondered, *Is he speaking to me, or to the hidden microphones he thinks are listening to us?*

"It wouldn't disturb you if I . . . stayed with you tonight?" she ventured uncertainly.

There was a long pause, then he answered, puzzled, "But you're married, aren't you? In fact, I seem to remember you have children."

She could not meet his gaze, but looked out the window, answering unsteadily, "I'm a widow. Don't you remember that?"

"No, I . . ."

"My children are dead, killed by the Ngaa. Don't you remember that, either?" Her eyes filled with tears. "Don't you remember how everything I'd worked so hard for, my whole carefully built-up life was incinerated in a single night? I envy you your amnesia. God, I wish I could forget! I wish I could forget it all!" The numbness that had gripped her since the fire was leaving at last, but leaving her with a pain she could hardly bear. She tore free of his fingers and threw herself face down on the bed, sobbing.

She felt Richard's hand on her heaving shoulder, heard him say, "I can't bring back what you've lost, but perhaps I can bring you revenge. The Ngaa is powerful, yes, but not omnipotent. I think I can kill it."

She rolled over and clutched him to her, crying, "No, Dick! Don't try to fight that thing alone. It will kill *you!*"

She desperately kissed his lips, but he was distant, his thoughts elsewhere. "It won't kill me," he said. "I know its weakness."

She thought, *He's planning already. . . .*

She kissed him again, and this time he returned her kiss. They made love half-dressed, as if afraid that there was no time, and when she left his room to go to her own she heard the guards locking his door.

The "attendant" looked up as J entered the room, then started to remove his headphones.

"No, no," said J. "I'm just checking in."

Disappointed, the attendant gestured toward the amplifier

107

on the table. "Nothing to check. Nothing to hear but snoring. Blade is sleeping like a drunken horse. Want to hear?"

"No, thanks."

"What time is it?"

J took out his pocketwatch and inspected it in the dim yellow light from the lamp on the bedtable, then answered, "A little after two."

"Isn't it odd, sir, how people think secret agents lead such exciting lives? They've no idea how bloody boring it is in reality."

"If they did we'd never be able to recruit anyone, would we?"

"I suppose not."

"Well, good night."

"Good night, sir."

J opened the door to the hall. The sanitarium was so silent the faint distant sounds of a freight train passing through Berkeley were clearly audible. J felt somewhat relieved now that some of his own men, flown in from London, had taken over the watch on Richard. Colby's men were not particularly bright, and one could never be frank with them.

"Wait, sir!" The attendant leaned forward intently.

J reentered the room and closed the door. "What is it?"

"Blade is talking in his sleep."

"If that's all . . ." J turned to leave.

"No, he's calling out, 'The Ngaa! The Ngaa!' and tossing and thrashing around. Give a listen."

"No, I don't think . . . well, all right."

J accepted the headphones and put them on.

He recognized Richard's murmuring voice, but could not understand what he was saying except for the one word Ngaa. The bedsprings were creaking and crashing violently.

Suddenly there was silence.

J was about to remove the headphones when he heard Blade speak again, this time clearly, like a man fully awake.

"The Ngaa," Richard said calmly, without fear.

Then J heard a sound he would hear again and again in nightmares for the rest of his life, the voice of the Ngaa, like the wind, like rustling trees, like a vast multitude of voices whispering in chorus: "Yes, we are the Ngaa."

"What do you want?" Richard challenged.

"Open the way for us. Let us come through."

"Never!"

"You are our entrance. Let us come through."

108

"No."

"We have served you well. We have removed your rival, made everything as it was long ago when you were happy. Now you must fulfill your side of the agreement."

"I made no agreement."

"You did! With your subconscious mind. We read your desires, listened to your unspoken prayers, and, because we are much like the being you call your God, we have answered. Is there something else you want? Do not speak. We will see it in your mind and obey. We will grant your wish, whatever it may be. But as we serve you, so must you serve us. Escape! We will help you. Return to London. Activate the computer and come to us. Help us to invade your dimension in all our power, to make our home on your world. Our planet is dead and our sun dying. Your planet is green and tempting. Your planet has air and water and living things. Come to us! Come!"

"No!"

The multitude of whispering voices grew fainter. "All you desire, in waking life or in dreams, we can give you. Come. Come." They were now scarcely audible.

Blade said, "Your time moves more quickly than mine, Ngaa, and your time is running out. I will not come to you. I will leave you in your crystal city in the sky, above the planet you have burned clean of life, leave you there to die."

The Ngaa answered with a fading sigh. "You will change your mind, Richard Blade, and soon."

When he heard nothing more, J removed the headphones. It was then he became aware that the hairs on the back of his hand were standing up and swaying. He glanced around, startled. The room was bathed for an instant in a dim blue glow.

The glow faded. The hairs on J's hand ceased moving. The Ngaa, as far as J could tell, was gone.

"Follow me," J commanded.

The attendant followed him into the hall, and down the passageway to the door of Richard's room.

"Richard!" J called. "Are you all right?"

"Yes, sir," came Richard's voice from inside.

J unlocked the door and, without waiting for an invitation, burst into the room. Blade had turned on the bedlamp and was sitting up, propped against his pillows, regarding J with amusement. "So, you did have my room bugged, didn't you?" Richard demanded.

"Of course I did!" J snapped. "Do you take me for an idiot? Was the Ngaa here just now?"

Richard nodded. "You heard the thing speak, didn't you?"

"I heard it," J said, annoyed. "I also heard that you spoke to it as if your memory had completely recovered."

"It has."

"And you didn't tell me?"

"The last link has only now fallen into place. I know why I could not remember. The Ngaa! The Ngaa spoke to me softly, there in the crystal city, repeating things to me over and over, showing me visions, or dreams, making me believe they were real. The Ngaa hypnotized me! That's the answer. The Ngaa hypnotized me to forget, then tried to hypnotize me to obey, but I would not. The Ngaa sent visions of horror, frightful nightmares drawn from my own subconscious, to try to force me to do as I was told, but I resisted. Somehow I resisted it."

J was puzzled. "You call the Ngaa *it*? Why not he or she?"

Richard chuckled. "Because the Ngaa is not a living being."

"Then what is it?"

"There is nothing like it in our dimension, but it is something like a disembodied spirit simulated by artificial means, and something like a . . . a computer."

Richard awoke with a feeling of smug satisfaction and lay a long time staring at the ceiling. Bright sunlight streamed in his window. Birds sang. Breakfast dishes clattered in the distance.

I've won, he thought.

Time was against the Ngaa. It would grow weaker and weaker, eventually losing its ability to manifest itself in the normal space-time continuum. Then, trapped in its own dimension where one Earth-minute was equal to many other-dimensional hours, the Ngaa would someday be destroyed by the nova of its sun.

Automatic victory!

A younger, more reckless Richard Blade might have been disappointed at the lack of "action" and adventure, but Blade had learned the value of a victory that did not deplete his resources, did not leave him less able to deal with the challenges of the future.

There was a knock at the door.

"Come in," Richard called.

The key rattled in the lock. J entered, returning the key to

110

his waistcoat pocket. "Good morning, Richard. You're looking well," the old man said, eyeing Blade thoughtfully.

"I'm feeling well," Richard replied, swinging his feet to the floor.

"Well enough to face a government examiner? Well enough to convince the fellow of your sanity?"

"A government examiner?" Richard stood up.

"Yes. Perhaps several. The Prime Minister has delivered an ultimatum: unless you are sane enough to pass his tests, he'll close down Project Dimension X for good. The deadline, I might add, is only four days away. In the meantime you are confined to quarters here. In particular you are under no circumstances to return to London or have anything to do with the KALI computer. Those are orders!"

Richard slipped on his usual white slacks and white T-shirt. "Sensible precautions, though hardly necessary. Why would I want to go near KALI? And even if I did want to, how would I escape from this snug little rabbit warren of yours? How would I transport myself all the way from here to England? Typically British of the PM to forbid me to do something I am both unwilling and unable to do."

"Glad you see it that way, old chap." J clapped Richard on the back. "You are completely recovered, aren't you?"

"Completely."

"Excellent! After breakfast I'll phone Downing Street and tell them to send their examiners straight away. We'll snatch the project from the jaws of oblivion at the last possible moment, in the style of the very best Victorian melodrama." J's usual reserve had been replaced by a surprising warmth and exuberance.

"And then it will be business as usual at the Tower of London, eh?" Richard frowned.

"Of course. What's wrong?"

"I don't think it would be wise to use KALI again for awhile. At least not with the same instrument settings."

"No? Because of the Ngaa?"

"Exactly. The Ngaa is powerful, dangerous and . . . desperate. Can we risk opening a gateway for it to reenter our dimension?"

"Definitely not."

The two men left the room together. Guards waited outside. Even now, though Richard was apparently his old self again, J took the absurd precaution of locking the door.

They went downstairs and entered the dining hall.

Richard looked around with a sudden uneasiness. "Where's Zoe?"

Colby, at the head table, glanced up and answered, "I haven't seen her this morning. She must still be in her room."

Richard wheeled and strode back the way he had come.

The guards tensed and reached for their tranquilizer pistols, but J signaled to them not to fire. Richard swept past them so quickly he almost knocked one of them over, then mounted the stairs three steps at a time. J, puffing and wheezing, followed him up.

Richard accosted an attendant who was coming down the hall outside Zoe's room. "Have you seen Mrs. Smythe-Evans?"

The man looked startled. "Why yes, I have."

"In her room?"

"No, she came out just a few minutes ago."

"Where did she go?"

"Down the back stairs, but it's certainly strange that you're asking me these things."

Richard shot him a worried glance. "Strange? Why?"

"It was you she was with, Mr. Blade."

Richard's smugness vanished, to be replaced with a sick apprehension. He brushed past the puzzled attendant and, breaking into a run, bounded down the back stairs. To the amazement of the kitchen staff, he sprinted past the stoves and refrigerators and burst through the screen door out onto the back porch.

Half-blinded by the sudden sunlight, he almost tripped and fell as he went down the steps, then paused, shading his eyes with his hands, searching the tennis courts and groves of pine and eucalyptus. No one was in sight.

"Damn," he whispered.

Then he heard a familiar laugh in the distance, from the front yard. *Her* laugh!

As the guards appeared, red-faced from running, on the back porch, Richard was off again, rounding the corner of the mansion at a long-legged lope.

Now he was in the side yard, now in the front, now pounding past the lion statues and the flagpole, across the weed-cracked paving stones toward the wire-mesh fence, toward the front gate where he could see green-uniformed armed guards turning to look in his direction.

Then he saw Zoe.

She was nearly to the front gate, walking with a jaunty

112

step, dressed in her borrowed white nurse's outfit, her back to him. At her side was a tall, muscular man in white slacks and T-shirt. Blade had no trouble recognizing the man.

"Myself," Richard whispered. He thought, *And yet not myself. The Ngaa!*

Richard cupped his hands around his mouth as he ran and shouted, "Zoe! Zoe! Stop!"

She stopped, turned to look back over her shoulder. Her eyes widened.

"Zoe!" Richard called. "Don't go with him!"

She looked first at Richard, then at the man beside her, confused.

The man turned, smiling with Richard Blade's face, smiling triumphantly. His hand shot out and grasped Zoe by the wrist. She screamed and tried to pull away.

Desperately Richard put on a burst of speed.

He had almost reached them when, with a sharp bang like a pistol shot, they vanished.

Howling, anguished, Richard hurled himself full-length on the pavement where they'd been standing, clutching at the coarse weeds that thrust themselves up through the cracks.

The weeds were black and crumbly, as if they'd been burned, and the surface of the stone in that one area was so hot it hurt his fingers.

In the air he could smell, faintly but distinctly, the acrid stench of ozone.

Chapter 11

The three men sat in Dr. Colby's office. The room was no longer dim, as it was during therapeutic sessions, but flooded with morning sunlight. Richard sat on the couch, Dr. Colby nearby in his usual chair, and J behind the heavy dark-stained desk.

Richard said, "What do you intend to do now, sir?" The question was addressed to J.

J sighed. "For the moment, nothing."

Richard stood up to face him angrily. "Nothing?"

"Calm down, Richard," the old man said soothingly. "We have our men combing the neighborhood, of course, but . . ."

"Your men? Is that all?" Richard advanced toward the desk. "What about the local authorities? The police? The FBI?"

"It's best we keep this to ourselves," J said tonelessly. "Some word of it might get back to the Prime Minister . . ."

Richard's fist crashed down on the desk, leaving a crack in the veneer. "What are you saying, J? That you're planning on keeping this a secret from the Prime Minister? That you won't even call on Copra House for assistance?"

J templed his fingers. "That is essentially correct. You understand . . ."

Richard broke in, "Yes, I understand. Any sort of bad news might influence the Prime Minister to shut down the project."

"Quite so," J admitted.

A new thought flashed into Richard's mind. "Or is there more to it? J, have you told the PM about the Ngaa?"

"Well, as a matter of fact, no." At last J's voice betrayed a hint of embarrassment.

Blade was angry. "I don't like this, J. I don't like it one damn bit."

"I didn't expect you to like it, Richard. I did, however, expect you to listen to reason." J looked up with troubled eyes at the giant looming over him. "Would it help, really, to broadcast our little problems all over the world? Think, my boy, think! Would all the police we could possibly summon find your Zoe if the Ngaa chose to keep her hidden?"

"Perhaps not." Richard's broad shoulders slumped.

J leaned forward. "Dr. Colby and I believe the Ngaa and Zoe are somewhere in the neighborhood. Isn't that right, doctor?"

Colby agreed quickly, "Yes, sir. It is Richard the Ngaa is trying to influence. The Ngaa will stay close to Richard, and keep Mrs. Smythe-Evans with it."

"Let me look for her," said Blade. "Set me free and let me look for her."

"That I cannot permit!" J spoke sharply. "You must stay here until the government examiners arrive, and then you must put on the most convincing performance of sanity for them that your mentality can conceive, and that's an order!"

Richard thought, *We shall see about that.*

"And not a word to them about the Ngaa," J added. "Is that understood?"

"Yes, sir," Richard responded.

J studied his face suspiciously. "You worry me more when you say yes than when you say no. You must realize that if we lose Zoe—and I don't think we will—she is one of us now. She's a soldier, like you and I, and expendable."

"Expendable. Yes, sir."

"So you will obey my orders?"

"To the letter, sir."

"I hope you won't take this personally, but I'm going to lock you in your room until the examiners arrive. A routine precaution, since you've given me your word . . ."

"Of course, sir. If I were in your place, I wouldn't believe me either."

Dr. Colby stifled a nervous laugh.

London and Berkeley have one thing in common: fog.

Berkeley's normal pattern was summer fog and winter rain, but the drought had made nonsense of normality and turned meteorology from a science into a gamble. The fog came now almost every night, though the season was all wrong for it, and instead of drifting in from the sea, it built up on cold windless evenings over the inland marshes east of the Berkeley hills, finally, in the frigid hours before dawn, spilling through the gaps in the coastal range to cascade in silent gray cataracts down upon the sleeping city and out toward the Golden Gate.

Richard lay on his bed, fully dressed and wide awake, watching the fog outside his window.

And snoring.

The snoring was for the benefit of J and whoever might be listening on the headphones down the hall. Was the fog thick enough yet? Yes. Soon it would start to thin again as the first rays of the morning sun burned it off.

The time to move was now.

Still snoring lustily, Richard rolled carefully out of bed and, on stocking feet, tiptoed to the door. He stopped snoring a second to listen, then proceeded to remove the hingepins from the hinges, first the top hinges, then the bottom.

He returned to his bed and picked up his pillowcase, from which the pillow had been removed. He put his tennis shoes in and lay down a moment, then rolled noisily, giving the impression to his listeners, he hoped, that he was turning onto his side.

Then he stopped snoring and waited.

Nothing happened.

He got up and once again padded noiselessly to the door. From his pocket he took a short length of wire he had earlier removed from the lightcord of his bedlamp. The wire was thin, no more than a few strands he had carefully separated from the rest, but he was sure it would be strong enough for his purposes.

He looped it around the door hinge and gently opened the door on the hinge side. The room, fortunately for him, had never been intended to hold a determined escapee. Colby had not bothered to change the hinges he had inherited from the ballet school that had been the building's previous tenant.

Richard squeezed through into the dimly lit hallway, then, pulling on the wire, drew the door back into its frame so that from the outside there was no way to tell the hingepins had been removed. Smiling, he pulled out the wire and pocketed it.

Still in stocking feet he moved swiftly to the door of the room where the tranquilizer pistols were kept. The combination padlock was no serious problem, though he missed the faint, almost imperceptible clicks of the falling tumblers the first time he tried, and had to spin the dial and start over. The second time it opened easily.

He entered the closet and found the pistols, six of them. With his bare hands he bent the barrel of each weapon slightly, enough to keep it from firing accurately, except for the sixth, which he left intact and dropped into his sack, along with several boxes of tranquilizer darts. *If these darts are intended for me,* he thought, *they'll be powerful, powerful enough to knock a man unconscious.*

Remembering that the guard would soon be coming to check his room, Richard left the closet and locked it quickly, then descended the back stairs into the pitch-dark kitchen. Guided mainly by memory he threaded his way through the stoves, tables and shelves to the pantry, where, again by memory (for he had watched everything that was happening even before he had begun to speak), he found the burglar alarm and shut it off.

Next he glided to the back door, unlocked it, and stepped out onto the porch.

So far so good!

He put on his tennis shoes, knotted his pillowcase bag to his belt, and proceeded softly down the steps. Crouching, he rounded the corner of the building, moved through the side yard and, after a pause to look and listen, continued into the front yard.

In the distance he could see a blob of indistinct light where the guards at the front gate were talking in low voices. Richard could not make out what they were saying, but their tone of boredom clearly showed they knew nothing of Richard's intentions. Richard checked the fog, the lighting. Some dim yellow light came from the front porch, but not enough to illuminate the thing that interested him.

The flagpole.

He darted across the weed-cracked paving stones to the base of the pole and gripped it firmly. It was better anchored than he'd expected, but three good tugs, with feet planted on either side of it, and it pulled free, making a scraping sound that Richard was afraid the guards might hear.

He paused, the pole swaying above him.

No, the guards went on talking in the same bored tone.

Richard, balancing the pole in his hands, sped across the paving stones toward the side fence. As he entered the grove of trees on one side of the walkway, he again relied on memory to guide him. In the darkness and fog his eyes were not much help. Up ahead must be the wire-mesh fence topped with barbed wire. Exactly how high had it been? Exactly where was it located? If he was going to vault it, he'd have to be high enough not to get caught in the barbed wire, but

117

low enough so he wouldn't fall back or, clearing the fence, break his neck on the other side.

He set the base of the pole on the ground, then lowered the shaft carefully, finding the point where he thought he should hold it. Here? No, here!

He lifted it, hefted it for balance. Yes, that felt right. He was now holding it parallel to the ground.

He advanced toward the unseen fence, careful not to strike anything with his awkward seesawing burden.

There was the fence, exactly where he'd expected it.

He measured it with his eye, then retreated for his run. It would have to be perfect the first time. It wasn't likely he'd get a second chance.

He wheeled, swinging the pole into position, took a deep breath, and started. Even now, running full tilt, he made very little noise, less noise than the distant guards, who now burst out in a gale of harsh laughter, as if at some particularly obscene joke.

The fence appeared out of the fog, looming ahead.

The point of Richard's pole dropped, dug into the ground. Richard, clinging to the pole, soared upward and, at the top of the arc, thrust the pole back and himself forward.

The barbed wire grazed his elbow as he plunged.

The ground, though he tried to do a parachutist's roll, socked him with the force of a wrecker's demolition ball, knocking the wind out of him, setting the universe spinning. Had it not been for the soft ground cover of pine needles, he could easily have cracked a rib.

On the other side of the fence the pole fell with a clatter that seemed deafening.

The conversation of the guards ceased.

A flashlight beam swung from side to side in the fog. One of the guards—perhaps both of them—was coming. Richard, rolling from his back to his belly, could hear the tramp of heavy boots. Yes, both of them were coming. He could tell by the sound.

Richard thought, *Shall I run for it?*

He realized he could not. He was still too dazed from the fall. He waited, hardly daring to breath.

The flashlight beam passed directly across the fallen pole and continued on. Didn't those idiots know this was no mere stick of wood? Didn't they notice the old flagpole was not in its usual place?

"Nothing here," said the first guard.

"Always a lot of funny noises around here at night. Maybe it was a deer. A lot of deer have been coming into town because of the drought. Nothing green out in the woods anymore," said the second.

"Yeah, right. It must have been a deer," agreed the first.

The two men turned and tramped back toward the front gate.

Richard exhaled.

When he felt able, he crept away, listening to the resuming bored conversation of the guards, and scaled a high wooden picket fence, dropping catlike into someone's backyard. From the yard he passed along the side of a stucco-faced cottage and found himself on a narrow winding street lined with parked cars with their wheels up on the curb, sparsely lit by fog-shrouded yellow streetlights.

"I can't believe it was so easy," Richard whispered to himself, as his previous anxiety was replaced with a rush of delighted exhilaration. He picked a direction and started to jog along at an effortless mile-eating pace, pausing to crouch in the bushes only when eyes or ears warned him of an approaching car.

When he had run what seemed to him at least three miles, he came in sight of a small two-story brown shingle-sided house where he could see, through the picture window, a flickering television screen.

He slowed to a walk, climbed the front steps, and pressed the doorbell. From the other side of the door he could hear some sort of beast roaring on the TV, and a woman screaming, then approaching footsteps.

A peephole opened at about eye level, and someone looked out. "Who is it?" demanded a gruff, weary voice.

Richard stood back so the man could see him, saying, "My name is Howard DeVore. I'm an ambulance driver. We've had an accident down the road. Could I use your phone to call in?"

"Well, eh, all right. I suppose so." The man grudgingly opened the door, after first unlocking a deadbolt lock and removing a door chain. "The phone's right here in the hall."

Richard entered, brushing past the man, glancing at him only long enough to notice that he was bald, middle-aged, and wearing a T-shirt decorated by a picture of Howard the Duck.

"I saw your light," Richard said.

119

"Yeah," the man answered with a yawn. "I couldn't sleep, so I stayed up to watch the Creature Feature show on the boob tube. You know how it is."

"Yes, I know how it is." Richard located the telephone and lifted the receiver.

The man hovered around, apparently hoping to listen in on the conversation.

"Do you mind?" Richard demanded acidly, and the man retreated into his front room, muttering. The television continued to roar and scream and play violent crashing symphonic chords.

Richard dialed a number, thinking, *It's been fifteen years. I hope they're still keeping this number going.*

The answer came on the second ring. "Tomcat Skip Tracer Service." The man's voice was cultured, slightly contemptuous. *Thank God,* thought Richard. But then he realized he needn't have worried. The Tomcat Skip Tracer Service was a wholly-owned clandestine subsidiary of the CIA. Once opened, a CIA front business never closes, no matter how little money it makes or how useless it is as an intelligence tool. The theory is that someday, somehow, it will come in handy.

"This is Richard Blade. I need help. Can you patch me through to Ordway?"

There was a silence, then the voice on the other end of the line said, "We haven't heard anything about you for a long time, Dick."

"You're not supposed to hear things about me if I'm doing my job right."

"You've got a point there. Okay, I'll put you through to Ordway, but for your sake I hope you're in deep trouble. If you're not, you will be. Ordway likes his beauty sleep."

In the small gymnasium with the disquieting mirrors J stood by the wall phone frowning, the yellowish naked light-bulb overhead accentuating his unhealthy complexion and the flaccid purple sacs under his eyes.

"Lord Leighton, is that you?" J demanded.

"Of course it's me. Who did you expect?"

"I don't know. I don't know. Listen, Leighton . . ."

"You sound upset, J old boy. Has there been some new disaster over there?"

J drew out his pocket handkerchief and clumsily mopped

120

his glistening brow. "Exactly. Two new disasters in fact."

"Give them to me one at a time, and pause in between. Let me savor the first to the full before I proceed to the second."

J noted with annoyance that Leighton's dry sense of humor, normally dormant, was becoming active under stress. "The first is Zoe. She has vanished."

"Run off somewhere, no doubt, to have a bit of fun."

"No, literally vanished—poof—before the eyes of witnesses."

"Some sort of shabby stage legerdemain, I'll wager. A cheap magic trick to make a fool out of you!"

"The magician, in this case, was the Ngaa."

"I see. That puts a different face on it, doesn't it? Has the Ngaa been up to any other tricks?"

"No, but isn't that enough?"

"You mentioned two disasters. What's the second?"

"Richard Blade has vanished, too."

"Poof? In front of witnesses?"

"No. He escaped."

Leighton began to chuckle. "Really? Right out from under the noses of the head of MI6 and a squad of our best cloak and dagger boys? Out of a high-security sanitarium? Tut tut!"

"It's not our fault. This place was never intended to hold someone like Blade. Damn! If only I'd insisted on a decent door on his room!"

"He would have gotten out anyway. You know that. It might have taken him ten minutes instead of five, or whatever it did take. Richard has never stayed very long anywhere he didn't want to stay, no matter how decent or indecent the doors."

"I suppose you're right, but you see, I'm sure, that this means a change of plans. We can't have those examiners from the Prime Minister's office coming here to examine Richard now."

"What do you expect me to do about it?"

"Stop them! Stall them somehow!"

"My dear boy, they're already on their way. I'll wager they're halfway across the Atlantic by now."

"Oh my God." J slumped against the wall.

"Are you turning religious on me? They say there are no atheists in the front lines, and we're in the front lines in a sense, aren't we?"

"Damn you, Leighton! How can you be so calm?"

"I've given up all hope. You should try it. Does wonders for the nerves."

"Given up? But . . ."

"If you're quite finished with your disasters, I'd like to tell you mine."

"No, not more . . ."

"Yes, more. The good Doctor Leonard Ferguson, he of the atrocious Hawaiian sport shirts, has come down with a fit of terminal patriotism, trotted over to Downing Street, and told all."

"Then the PM knows . . ."

"About the Ngaa? Yes."

"Oh my God."

"There you go again, J. You're beginning to worry me."

"The Prime Minister, Leighton! How did he react?"

"As we expected. He's shutting down the project, and please spare me your habitual blasphemies. You can forget about that deadline. You can forget the entire matter. In slightly more than twenty-four hours the PM's bully boys will be here with sledgehammers to smash KALI and everything else in the underground laboratory into very small bits. And what do I intend to do about it? Absolutely nothing. I am drinking, J. I am drinking the most excellent brandy. When the PM's men arrive, I venture to predict that I will be either unconscious or dead or, at worst, in an advanced and dignified state of delirious inebriation. I highly recommend to you, sir, a similar course of action. As to our friend Richard Blade, I suggest you quite simply call the police and whatever other local sheriffs, deputies, U.S. marshals and unwashed vigilantes, who are entrusted with the administration of justice out there on the western frontier. Let them turn their hounds to the chase! I'm sure they'll run Richard to ground in no time."

"But the question of security . . ."

Leighton laughed outright. "Security? Why my dear old friend, security assumes we have some secret left to keep!" J clearly heard the scientist sip and swallow.

"Yes, yes, you're quite right, of course." J suddenly felt weary and incredibly old. He thought, *With the project dead, how long will Leighton live?*

Leighton demanded, "Have you anymore nasty news to disturb an old man's well-earned retirement?"

"Well, no."

"Then with your permission I'll ring off."

Abruptly the phone went dead.

Numbly J held the receiver unitl it began to make impolite noises, then he hung up.

He thought, *Leighton's right. I should call the police.* An all-points bulletin would probably lead to Richard's arrest within hours. After all, Richard could not leave the country without a passport or money, and in that absurd white T-shirt and white slacks he would be highly conspicuous anywhere outside of Berkeley. True, Richard was armed, but only with an air-powered tranquilizer dart pistol that couldn't hit anything more than fifteen or twenty feet away. Richard could not get far. In fact, he was probably still skulking somewhere in the neighborhood.

For a moment J considered the notion that Richard might somehow get back to London. But how? And if he did manage to reach London, there was no way he could get into the underground project, and if he did get into the underground project, it would be too late. He'd find nothing there but wreckage.

Still, if Richard thought the Ngaa had taken Zoe back to its own dimension . . . J shrugged and thrust the thought from his mind. It returned, stronger than before. Yes, Richard might very well try to get back to London, and . . .

Suddenly J realized that there was one way Richard might succeed.

He closed his eyes, reaching far back in his mind for a telephone number he had not called in fifteen years.

Hoping he had it right, he dialed.

The voice came, "Tomcat Skip Tracer Service."

"This is J of MI6. Could you patch me through to Ordway?"

The man took it in his stride. "Right away, sir."

J heaved a sigh of relief, congratulating himself on a good memory. There were several clicks, then the sound of a telephone being rung. Ordway, of course, would not be in the same building with the Skip Tracer Service. Ordway could be literally anywhere in the world.

"Yes?" The voice on the other end was familiar, a soft, almost gentle baritone, with a hint of a Southern accent.

"Is this Ordway?"

"Ordway speaking."

"This is J of MI6."

"Yes. I recognized your voice. I had a report you were in

123

the Bay Area. You're up at Saxton Colby's shabby excuse for a sanitarium, aren't you?"

"Why yes, that's right." Ordway always had been a show-off, like most of those CIA bastards. A British agent would never have revealed that he knew J was in the region. A British agent would have made sure the flow of information was all one way.

"I thought you'd phone when you had time. Want to have supper with me? Talk over old times?" Ordway was charming as always. Charming, charming, charming! Yet somehow never quite a gentleman.

"No," J answered, trying to be even more charming. "I'm calling about a bit of a problem we're having."

"A problem?"

"You remember Richard Blade? The chap who was with me when I was here last?"

"I'll never forget him. He was *some* kind of agent."

"Yes. Quite. We've had him here at Colby's for examination and—er—treatment."

"You don't say. Hey, that sounds bad."

"It's nothing serious. We were doing some deprogramming. I should say, we were treating some—er—battle fatigue." J felt a flush of embarrassment. He did not like lying about Blade, but was fairly sure the whole truth would not be believed. His compromise lacked the conviction of either sincerity or a well-crafted fabrication.

"I'm sorry, but I don't . . ."

"The long and short of it, Ordway, is that he has broken out and we have to get him back. He might hurt someone or himself. He's not altogether right in the head, you know."

"I see."

"It struck me that since he was an old friend of yours, so to speak, he might try to contact you."

"That seems reasonable."

"Well, has he?"

"No."

"If he does, will you call me?"

"Of course."

"I'll give you my number."

"I have it already, if you're still at the sanitarium."

"Yes, I am, and could you put out the word? Could you get your men to dig around for him? I have his picture and fingerprints."

"So do I."

J thought, *Damn showoff. Always was a damn showoff.* But J's voice, when he spoke, was nothing but charming. "Don't hurt him, Ordway, but bring him in as soon as you can."

"You can count on me."

"Thank you, sir."

"Think nothing of it, J old buddy. I'm happy to be working with you again."

After hanging up, J stood a while in thought before gathering the moral force to dial.

"Information," chirped the operator.

"Give me the number of the Berkeley police department."

Glen Ordway of the CIA turned pensively away from the phone and regarded his guest, who lounged in a black leather-upholstered overstuffed chair under a Picasso cubist painting.

"What'll you have?" Ordway smiled broadly.

"Brandy and soda," answered Richard Blade.

Chapter 12

Glen Ordway was a small, wiry mulatto, an ideal racial mix for intelligence work in a world where, increasingly, almost all the serious action was in the so-called Third World. Ordway could be an African among Africans, an Arab among Arabs, a moorish Spaniard among Spaniards, a South American among South Americans, even an Oriental among Orientals or an Italian among Italians. He needed no makeup, only a change of language and mannerisms, and he spoke, Richard knew, twenty-seven languages and acted with virtuoso aplomb in all of them. He was now in the United States, and therefore spoke, acted and looked exactly like an American ghetto Black, at least when out on the streets of East Oakland where he maintained this apartment near the Bay Area Rapid Transit line.

His neighbors, if they noticed him at all, must have taken him for a rhythm-and-blues musician, or perhaps a successful pimp, in his light-blue slacks, dark-blue blazer, white silk shirt, platform shoes and cat's-eye sunglasses.

"Your drink, Mr. Blade," Ordway said, and his accent was shifting, becoming British. As usual, almost unconsciously, Ordway was absorbing the speech and mannerisms of the person he was with.

"Thank you, Glen." Blade accepted the glass. "And not just for the drink." He glanced at the white pushbutton phone on Ordway's modern black steel desk.

"You did not wish to be found, therefore you will not be found." Ordway had mixed himself a whiskey sour. He raised it in a toast. "To the confusion of MI6."

They clinked glasses and sipped.

"I hope this won't cause trouble for you," Blade said.

"No trouble. There's no love lost between the CIA and The Old Firm." The Old Firm was standard jargon for the British Secret Intelligence Services. "My station chief will probably award me ten brownie points when he hears about

126

this. He and I agree on many things, including the opinion that your boss is a pompous ass long overdue to be taken down a peg. Besides, I owe you a favor."

"For what?"

"You remember that night in the North Beach district of San Francisco? You remember that dude who was dressed up as a woman that you were after?"

Richard nodded. "I remember."

Glen chuckled and went on. "We tracked him into the ladies john in Miss Prisford's Tea Room. Good old Miss Prisford's! You could buy anything there, animal, vegetable or mineral, except tea. I busted in and looked around and didn't see anybody right away, and you followed me in and— blam blam blam—shot that fruit right through the wall of his toilet stall. When he fell out on the cement this cute little pistol went bouncing across the floor. It was a Baretta, wasn't it?" Glen's accent became more American.

"That's right."

"I knew it! I forget names and faces, but I never forget a gun. Well, that fruit could very easily have canceled my pension, if you know what I mean. *I* didn't see the bastard! I still to this day don't understand how you spotted him."

"I heard him."

"Sure, but how did you know he wasn't a genuine lady in there?"

"A true lady does not stand on the toilet seat in order to prevent her feet from showing."

Glen drained his glass and went over to the black-upholstered bar for a refill. "I remember the gun you used. It was a German job, wasn't it? A big Walther PPK pistol with an eagle and swastika embossed on the handle. A Nazi gun! I've always wondered where you got it."

"I picked it up from its original owner when he had no more use for it. I still own the thing, though I haven't had occasion to use it for years."

"A beautiful weapon," Glen murmured reverently.

"A classic," Richard agreed, raising his glass.

Silently they toasted the Walther PPK.

"So you see," Glen went on, after wiping his mouth with the back of his wrist, "I might very well owe my life to you. You were there at the right time doing the right thing."

"I remember." Richard had to smile.

"So as I said, I owe you a favor. I assume you're planning on dropping out of sight for a while. Fine! I can get you a new passport and papers with a new name and a new past. Our plastic surgeons can give you a new face, if you need one. And if you're job hunting, the Company can use a man like you. Where would you like to surface? South America? Europe? Africa?"

Blade looked up at him, still smiling, and said softly, "England."

"England? Are you crazy, man?" Glen's accent went pure ghetto Black. "I mean, like, you gotta be puttin' me on!"

Richard said quietly, "Yes, England, as close to London as can be arranged."

"You know, I believe you. It's just crazy enough . . ."

"I can understand your misgivings, but I assure you I know exactly what I'm doing."

"You're walking like a lamb right into the mouth of the British lion."

"It can't be helped. There's something I must do."

The mulatto shrugged. "So be it. It will take a week for me to have your false papers prepared and to get you a plane ticket."

"I don't have a week."

"When do you want to leave?"

"Today."

"But the false papers . . ."

"I won't need them."

"The tickets . . ."

"With your help, I won't need them either."

"But how . . . ?"

Richard stood up. "I understand you fly regular spy plane missions over Russia from somewhere around here to the American airbase outside London."

Glen looked at him oddly, head cocked to one side. "You're not supposed to know about that, Dickie baby."

"Once in a while, by chance, MI6 blunders onto something. I want to hitch a ride on that plane. Can you arrange it?"

There was a long silence, then Glen said softly, "Yes, I can arrange it. Do you want a two-way ride?"

Richard did not meet the shorter man's intent gaze. "No, Glen. I rather expect this will be a one-way trip."

Richard Blade caught his first glimpse of the spy plane from the air, as Glen circled the desert airfield.

"What do you think of her?" Glen demanded, half-turning in the cockpit to look back over his shoulder at Richard.

"Not bad," Richard answered over the rushing roar of their jet fighter.

Moments later they touched down and taxied up to the looming bulk of a giant bomber. The spy plane was perched on the back of the bomber as if it were the bomber's child. Unlike the parent, who was unpainted save for the insignia of the U.S. Air Force, the child was painted a dull black and bore no markings of any kind. Glen brought his jet to a stop in the shadow of the larger plane's wing, cut the engines, unplugged himself, pushed back the canopy, and clambered out. Richard followed.

"Hi, Glen!" A groundcrewman in brown coveralls waved a greeting.

Glen jumped from his wing to the ground. "Hi, man."

The groundcrewman gestured toward the spy plane. "We waited for you. I hope you realize this puts us ten minutes behind schedule."

"What's ten minutes?" Glen retorted, grinning.

Richard jumped to the ground and looked around, noticing for the first time the nearby camouflaged bunkers that apparently were the airfield's only structures, at least the only structures above ground. He realized, with professional admiration, that once the field was cleared of aircraft, it would be completely invisible from above and almost invisible even from the ground. As far as he could see in all directions there was nothing but desert, except for some indistinct blue mountains on the horizon that shimmered dreamlike in the heat. There was not a breath of breeze, and the silence was so absolute that the crunch of his boots in the sand seemed like a desecration. He removed his crash helmet and wiped his sweating forehead with the back of his arm.

Glen introduced him to the groundcrewman. "Richard Blade, Mark Williams."

Richard pulled off a glove. The handshake was slippery with sweat. Richard was beginning to wish he'd kept his white T-shirt and slacks, instead of exchanging them for the olive drab coveralls Glen had loaned him. Of the things he had brought with him from the sanitarium, he now retained only the incongruous pillowcase containing the tranquilizer gun. This he gripped in his left hand like a trick-or-treat bag.

"Let's get this show on the road," Williams growled, with a frowning glance at his wristwatch.

"Right." Glen started for the ladder that extended from the bottom of the bomber, near the center of the fuselage.

The three men clambered up into the belly of the plane, and on up another ladder into the smaller plane above it.

Glen introduced Richard to the pilot. "Richard Blade, Chris Rasmussen." Rasmussen looked at Richard briefly but did not offer to shake hands. It was not difficult to see that Rasmussen regarded him as an unwelcome intruder.

Ordway helped Richard strap down and plug in. His seat was directly behind Rasmussen's, and there were no other seats, though the interior was surprisingly roomy. Rasmussen bent over the instruments, apparently too busy to pay any attention to his unwanted passenger.

Ordway gave Richard a clap on the back for luck, then, together with Williams, scrambled down through the floor.

A few minutes later the bomber was airborne, the spy plane still riding piggyback. Richard leaned over to watch, through the canopy, the grotesque dwindling shadow of the double aircraft rushing across the dunes. Over the low drone of the bomber's jets, he heard, in his helmet headphones, Ordway's cheery voice. "Mark and I are down here in the Mama bird. Everything okay, Blade?"

"No problems," Richard responded.

"All systems go," Rasmussen added.

They went into a steep bank, then began climbing.

Ordway went on, "This is the last thing I'll be able to say to you for the time being, old sock." His accent had gone British again. "In a few shakes Mama bird will kick Baby bird out on his own. We don't ever talk to Baby on the radio, since Baby isn't supposed to exist."

"I understand," said Richard.

Ordway's voice became more serious. "There's a pub in London called the Globe. Have you ever been there?"

"Once or twice," Blade said.

"If you ever want to contact me, leave a message at the Globe. They'll get it to me within eight hours."

"I'll remember that, Glen."

"Any questions?"

"There is one." Richard hesitated. "Why are you trusting me like this? I mean, how do you know . . ."

"That you're you? That you're okay?"

"Exactly."

"They took your voiceprint from your phone call at the Tomcat Skip Tracer Service and matched it with one we had on file from your last visit. And all the time you were talking at my place, your voice was being checked for the stress

130

patterns of a liar by our resident electronic wizard in the next room. And of course your fingerprints were on your brandy and soda glass. They checked that after we left. But mainly, you knew the reason why that fruit in the john wasn't a lady."

"You don't miss a trick, do you, Ordway?"

"We try to stay on top, chum." The accent had slipped all the way into a rich cockney. "Well, cheerio, pip pip, and ta ta, Dickie, me lad."

"Ta, ta, Glen," said Richard, half-laughing.

From this point on the intercom was taken over by a crisp, alert, but calm interchange between the pilot of the bomber and Rasmussen, the pilot of the spy plane. Without being able to see the instruments, Richard estimated that they were between seven and eight miles high, in the lower stratosphere. The sky had gradually changed from blue to near-black. The sun had brightened, but when he looked away from it, he could begin to see the stars. The few clouds, thin and stringy, were below him. The cabin, in spite of pressurization and heating, had cooled rapidly.

Rasmussen began counting down. "Ten, nine, eight . . ."

At the end of the count there was a lurch and the cockpit swayed in a way it could not have done when the two aircraft were linked. Baby was on his own!

The bomber swung into view to Richard's right, waving its wings in farewell.

Rasmussen returned the parting salutation, pressed a red button on the instrument panel, and eased forward the throttle at his side. The spy plane's own engines ignited and Richard was pressed forcefully into his seat by the sudden acceleration.

"How high are we going, Rasmussen?" Richard said into his helmet microphone.

"High enough," came the laconic reply on the earphones.

The plane was climbing much more rapidly than it had when attached to the mothership. Richard felt the vibration rise, then, with a shudder, they broke through the sonic barrier and the noise level, which had become too loud for conversation, dropped to a gentle drone and hiss, and even this hiss was dying away as, with increasing altitude, the atmosphere outside grew steadily thinner.

"May I ask a question?" Richard was trying to be friendly.

Rasmussen did not answer.

Richard persisted. "What does this plane do?"

"We take pictures," said Rasmussen.

"But can't you take pictures from an orbiting satellite?"

"Not good pictures."

This was the last thing either man said for the remainder of the flight. Richard contented himself with watching. The leading edges of the stub wings were heating up, glowing a dull red, but they began to fade again before any damage was done. The acceleration pressure continued for a while longer, then, as Rasmussen eased off the throttle, the pressure vanished, to be replaced by the unforgetable sensation of free fall, of weightlessness. In a moment they were drifting, without power, in the most total silence Richard had ever experienced. He could hear his own heartbeat, his own blood pulsing in his ears, his breathing and the other man's, the faint creaks of the ship adjusting itself to the vacuum of space. The temperature in the cockpit had become uncomfortably cold, and moisture was condensing on every bit of bare metal in sight, though something—probably wires imbedded in the plastic—kept the canopy from clouding.

There was a thump and Blade saw two large torpedolike objects fall away, turning slowly. He thought, *Expended fuel tanks. Probably fall into the Pacific or burn up on reentry.*

Reentry!

Reentry for the spy ship would come somewhere over Europe. If MI6 had not been misled, the entire flight would take slightly over an hour. In minutes he would be in England again!

He leaned as close as he could to the canopy and was rewarded by a glimpse of the coastline of Russia, almost unrecognizable beneath a swirl of white clouds.

He sat back with a sigh and closed his eyes, resting for the ordeal ahead. For a moment he was relaxed, on the verge of sleep, then he thought of Zoe. *I'm coming for you, Zoe. I'm coming, love.*

He thought of the Ngaa.

A terrible anger possessed him, driving away sleep, the most frightful fury he had ever known.

He thought feverishly, *I'm coming for you, Ngaa!*

Was it his imagination? Or did he hear a voice like a multitude of voices whispering in unison, whispering at the edge of his consciousness?

I'm waiting.

Chapter 13

As he had done before, times without number, the quaint red-clad chief Yeoman Warder marched his troop of four similarly dressed guards toward the looming fog-shrouded Bloody Tower, ancient lantern held high. A small crowd of tourists, Germans in short pants and green-feathered caps, looked on with mild boredom.

The sentry challenged the Warder. "Halt!"

"Detail halt!" the Warder commanded.

His men obeyed with mechanical precision.

"Who goes there?" said the sentry.

"Keys," said the Warder.

"Whose keys?" said the sentry.

"Queen Elizabeth's keys," said the Warder.

"Advance Queen Elizabeth's keys," said the sentry. "All's well."

"Present arms!" commanded the Warder.

His men obeyed.

The Warder doffed his ornate Tudor bonnet, calling out, "God preserve Queen Elizabeth!"

The guards responded, "Amen!"

From out of the darkening mists came the tolling of a bell. Ten o'clock. A bugler blew the Last Post. The Bloody Tower was locked. The strange eternal pageant of the Tower of London was officially over for another day.

As the squad marched off toward the Queen's House, the German-speaking tour guide began shepherding his tourists toward the exit.

When the Germans were at last gone the unobtrusive silent men of MI6 appeared from the shadows and took up their nightly vigil.

Casually they passed the word, seeming to stand a moment together now and then by pure chance.

"This is our last night here."

"The project is closing down tomorrow."
"It's all over."

Richard Blade's rowboat drifted slowly on the black River Thames, under the Cannon Street Station railroad bridge. A train, its lights only dimly visible, rumbled by overhead. He had heard the bells toll ten. He knew the tourists and Yeoman Warders had left, but he did not bend to the oars, did not try to hasten the little craft's progress. All too soon he would have to draw upon every muscle in his body, every nerve, every braincell.

He drifted, and rested, turning with the tide.

The railroad bridge faded in the gray haze behind him.

Ahead lay London Bridge, now marked only by a stream of slow-moving headlights and a harsh chorus of auto horns. The fog thinned slightly, and for a moment he could see on his right the outline of Southwark Cathedral silhouetted against a dull pink sky. Only a moment, then the fog closed in again.

He shivered. The heavy overcoat he was wearing could not quite cope with the cold, though thank God there was no wind. Under the coat he wore only a pair of swimming trunks. His body was smeared from head to foot with black oil, which gave very little protection against the weather, but made him less visible.

He looked down at his equipment, a shadowy pile in the bottom of the boat. There was his tranquilizer gun, still in its pillowcase bag. It was no Walther PPK, but it took more kindly to a dunking than any orthodox pistol. Its darts were propelled by compressed air, so it would be more reliable and quieter. Yes, a quiet weapon was important in this situation, where everything depended on surprise. Lastly, it was not a killing weapon. Richard did not want to kill his own comrades.

And there were his skin-diver's flippers, weighted belt and mask; all a gift, like the rowboat, from the CIA.

This was all he had, but to him it seemed enough.

He removed one of the oars from its oar lock and silently dipped it into the water behind the boat, using it as if it were a sculling paddle. He could not afford even the small sound of a creaking oar lock. The boat responded, began moving toward the left bank. He paused between strokes, letting it glide.

London Bridge passed overhead, and the stench of exhaust

fumes temporarily replaced the normal salt sea smell, the unique aroma of a river that felt the ebb and flow of the ocean tides this far from the sea.

He glanced up as he emerged beyond the bridge. A young man and a young woman were looking down at him from the rail, but they were interested, it seemed, only in each other. The fog swallowed them up as Richard sculled and paused, sculled and paused. Drops of water fell from the oar shaft, making clusters of expanding circles that slid away behind.

For the hundredth time he reviewed his plan.

Oddly enough it was not a new, fresh scheme, hatched for this occasion, but an old scheme, or a variation of an old scheme. For years Richard had amused himself by working out ways for stealing the Crown Jewels, safely lodged—or so everyone supposed—in the Wakefield Tower, directly behind the secret entrance to Project Dimension X. He had never seriously considered putting these larcenous plots into motion, but he had often wistfully reflected, *England lost a good cracksman the day I tipped me for MI6.*

He knew, for example, the habits of the MI6 ops who did night duty at the Tower of London, knew that they checked the actual Traitor's Gate only once every half-hour, knew that, though he had mentioned it several times, the guards had not understood how vulnerable the Tower of London was from the river side. To them the river was as good as a wall; to Richard the river was as good as a wide-open entrance.

He knew also that, from their usual stations, the ops could not see Traitor's Gate.

He frowned as the fog cleared slightly.

They *could* scan the river.

On the right bank the cruiser H.M.S. *Belfast* materialized, a floating museum permanently moored to Symon's Warf. To his left appeared the Tower Pier, with its tour boats. Beyond the pier he could begin to see the floodlit central White Tower surrounded by the darker lesser towers of the Tower of London complex.

And he could see, near what must be the Traitor's Gate, two moving lights. Flashlights! They were moving away from the gate. The guards must have completed their half-hourly inspection. Richard congratulated himself on his timing.

He could see the guards. Could they see him?

Probably not. He could see only their lights, and he was carrying no lights.

The fog thickened again. He knew the boat could carry him no further without attracting attention. The time had come for a little swim.

He took off his overcoat. Instantly his teeth began to chatter.

He put on the weighted belt, then the flippers, then the mask, which covered his eyes and nose but not his mouth. He knotted the sack containing his tranquilizer gun to his swimming trunks. As he worked, he breathed deeply, again and again, building up the oxygen content of his blood until he was slightly dizzy.

Then, steeling himself, he crept to the rear of the boat and slowly, carefully lowered himself overboard. The Thames was cold with a bite that was actually painful, but he forced himself to bear it.

The floodlighted White Tower was becoming visible again, closer than before. He took his bearings on it, sucked one last gulp of air into his lungs, then dove, bending at the waist, ducking his head downward, and raising his feet in the air.

In the darkness under the surface there was no way to tell direction. He moved like a programmed robot, following a prearranged course, trusting to memory to supply what the senses could not. He had, he knew, slightly more than one minute before he would have to surface. He swallowed, equalizing the pressure.

With vigorous kicks he set off in what he hoped was the right direction.

How would he know when he had gone far enough? Each of us has an inborn sense of time, and Richard Blade had developed his, learned to depend on it. If the time-sense failed, there were his lungs. His lungs would tell him when he could go no further.

There was a vague saltiness in the water.

He paid little attention to that, only to the cold.

The cold!

He had not realized that it would be so numbingly, horribly cold. Fragmentary pictures flashed through his mind. Penguin Club swimmers diving through holes cut in the ice. How long did they stay in the water? Nazi experiments with cold during World War II. How long did the victims survive? These were things Richard suddenly wished he had studied more carefully, wished he had added to his vast store of trivia.

His sense of time said, "One minute." He unbuckled his weighted belt and let it drop, then drifted, not moving a muscle, letting his natural buoyancy lift him slowly, all too slowly, toward the surface.

His head broke water!

He rolled onto his back and inhaled joyfully once, twice, three times, while he took his bearings.

Yes, he was near the Tower embankment.

Yes, he was sheltered by that embankment from the view from the probable location of the guards.

Thank God, he thought, and went on breathing.

In the distance he could see his boat, almost invisible in the darkness and fog. The current would soon take it far downriver. He turned onto his belly, breathing more normally, and treaded water. He too was drifting, drifting beyond the place where he'd hoped to land. He thrust his feet downward.

As he'd expected, there was sand down there.

Smiling, though he was shivering uncontrollably, he waded against the current.

There, exactly where he'd expected it, was the Queen's Stair leading up out of the water. He sat on a step, just above the water level, and removed his flippers and mask. He would need them no longer. He lowered them noiselessly into the black water and let them go.

When he felt he had fully recovered his wind, he started up the stairs. At the top, he knew, he would be exposed, but not for long.

At the head of the stairs he crouched, waiting for the fog to thicken, listening for the guards. There was nothing to be heard but the usual murmuring roar of the city and an occasional auto horn. He raised his head and peered around.

The fog closed in.

He sprang up and ran, clutching his tranquilizer pistol so it wouldn't bang on his thigh. He glimpsed a few leafless trees, an ancient cannon pointed riverward, then he was over the rail and into the filled-in moat. Keeping low, he padded toward St. Thomas's Tower, where he vaulted another fence and found himself in the broad archway of the Traitor's Gate, leaning against the massive grillwork.

He listened.

Nothing.

He looked around.

Nothing but slow-moving mist.

He located the heavy combination padlock at the center of the gate, dangling from a length of chain. Richard knew the ways of padlocks! He set to work.

One tumbler. Two.

It was easy, particularly since, having once seen the lock opened, he had a fair idea of the combination already.

The lock released on the first try.

He opened the ponderous gate, and it creaked. Had anyone heard? Apparently not. He slipped inside and resecured the chain, relocked the padlock.

In the yellow light from a single bare bulb in the ceiling, he crossed the inner chamber and located the secret door. It opened easily.

He passed through and trotted along the dim damp tunnel beyond, through the maze of subbasements, on to the familiar elevator door.

Would his thumbprint still be stored in the computer's memory banks? Why not? Everyone thought he was on the other side of the planet. Why would they bother to change the banks?

He pressed the elevator button firmly, letting the button read his print, wondering what he would do if the computer rejected him.

With a swish the elevator arrived and opened.

Richard stepped inside. The door slid shut.

As the elevator plunged downward, he opened the mouth of his pillowcase bag, wondering, *Will there be someone on duty at the entrance to the complex, next to the elevator door?* Sometimes there was and sometimes there wasn't. Special Services had become rather lax in the placement of its human guards for years now, putting too much confidence in super-sophisticated electronic devices. Richard had warned them about that, but nobody had listened. Now he would give them a demonstration.

The elevator slowed to a stop. The heavy bronze door rolled open.

There was someone on duty, sitting at the olive drab desk in the brightly-lit foyer, reading a magazine, a lean fellow in green coveralls. As he looked up, surprised, Richard recognized him as Bill Jemison, one of Lord Leighton's techmen.

"Hello, Bill," Richard said casually, stepping from the elevator into the welcome warmth of the underground installation. The door closed behind him.

"Well, if it isn't Richard Blade," Jemison answered. "I didn't know you were back from the states."

"Leighton called me back for a mission." Richard noted that there was an intercom unit on Jemison's desk. It would not do for Jemison to punch a button on that unit and give the alarm.

"I see you're already greased up," said Jemison.

"That's right."

"I'm glad to see you looking so well. I heard the last trip was a rough one. Ferguson told me you might be hospitalized for a long while."

Good old Ferguson, Richard thought with irony. He said, "It wasn't as bad as they thought. I'm fine now."

Jemison leaned back with a sigh. "So it's one last mission, eh, before they close down the show? It'll have to be a quick one if you're going to be back before the PM's boys come in the morning to pull our plug once and for all."

"In the morning? Yes, quite." This was the first Richard had heard of the new deadline, but he did not let his surprise show. Inwardly he was asking himself, *Does that change my plans? No, I can't let it.*

Jemison said, "I'll tell Lord Leighton you're here." He leaned forward, reaching for the intercom button.

Richard snatched the tranquilizer pistol from its sack and pulled the trigger. There was a snick like the small explosive hiss of an angry cat. The dart lodged in Jemison's neck.

Jemison looked toward Richard with amazement, then his eyes clouded and he began to slip forward out of his chair. Richard sprang forward and caught him, carefully lowering him onto the desk, head pillowed on arms. *They'll think you're asleep,* Richard mused with grim amusement. *That's nothing unusual around here.* Still, someone might appear at any moment and try to wake him, and then all hell would break loose.

Richard sprinted from the foyer and down a series of long door-lined corridors. Even for this late hour, the rooms along the hall were unusually silent, as if the project had already shut down. Why would anyone work, knowing it was all for nothing?

But the electronic sensors were still on duty no doubt, tracking his every step, weighing him, measuring him, listening to his heartbeat, his breathing, identifying him as one of those few men who could walk these passageways without setting off an alarm. At the end of the final passage a massive door slid open, cued by the electronic surveillance system, and he entered the central computer complex.

The tiny blinking lights on the consoles indicated that the computers were not active, but were on standby. The lighting in the room was muted, but he could make out a glint of chrome here, a smooth plastic surface there, a maze of matt green cabinets covered with dials, switches and lights, with an occasional cathode ray tube, green-glowing like an otherworldly television screen.

Abruptly Richard was startled by an animalistic snort and wheeze, amplified and echoed by the bare rock walls. A snore! Richard advanced and found, awkwardly sprawled in a chair before a readout unit, the dwarfish twisted form of the hunchbacked Leighton. On the worktable of the readout unit stood three empty bottles. There were other bottles on the floor. The air was filled with the reek of alcohol.

Richard stepped closer. There was a sheet of diagram paper on the table and several pencils. Had Leighton been working on something as he drank? Richard read the heading: "KALI program 280." Richard had never learned how to program computers, but over the years he had learned to read some parts of Leighton's planning sheets. His eye scanned the columns, looking for something that would identify the purpose of this program.

He found it.

In the place set aside for the height and weight of the person to be sent into the X dimensions, Richard found not his own specifications, but Leighton's. Leighton had been working on a program to send himself into the X dimensions! This frail old man was planning to launch himself on a journey that brought madness and death to voyagers who were young and strong. And if he survived, how could he return after the PM closed down the project? But of course! Lord Leighton did not want to return. With his beloved project ended, what was left for him in this world?

Noiselessly Richard passed the sleeping scientist and continued on.

The massive vault door of KALI's inner sanctum, her holy of holies, opened itself and stood open, waiting for him. Richard entered with a feeling of awe. The door swung shut. For the first time in his life, Richard was alone with the computers, without J, without the gnomelike Leighton. He seemed to sense, as he could never sense before, the presence of something . . . no, *someone*. The computer had perhaps been a mere machine once, when the project had begun, but now it was more. Where is the line that divides mechanical computation from conscious thought? Who can say? Richard only knew that somewhere, sometime in the years they'd been working on Project Dimension X, that line had been crossed without them noticing it.

KALI was not a thing.

KALI was a person.

Like a worshipper approaching an altar, Richard approached the control console. A small red light shone like a ruby eye above the only two switches that were active, the Program Stop and the Program Start. KALI was on standby. She was waiting for him. He laid aside his tranquilizer pistol. He knew she would not transport it. He slipped off his swimming trunks. He knew from experience they would not follow him into the worlds beyond the gateway, into other spacetime continuums, other universes. Only naked would she take him. Only naked would she give him a new birth on a different plane of existence.

He glanced at the box in which he would stand when he was launched. How like a coffin it was! And at the same time, how like a womb. Its copper-colored many-segmented interior gleamed in the subdued light. It stood open, waiting.

Like a hand. Like a mouth. Like a Venus's-flytrap.

Richard hesitated no longer, but stepped forward and firmly pressed Program Start. The red light went out. A green-glowing digital clock lit up and began the countdown.

He crossed to the center of the room, to the wire-bedecked sarcophagus, as KALI inexorably raced through her preliminary sequences.

He stepped inside, leaned back against the cold metal, and thought about the Ngaa. *I'm coming, Ngaa. Nothing stands in my way now.*

And he thought of Zoe. He thought of Zoe for a long time.

The clock went on flickering, moving into the low numbers. Fourteen. Thirteen. Twelve.

Suddenly Richard heard the vault door open with a swish. He turned his head.

Lord Leighton was standing in the doorway, swaying drunkenly.

Behind his thick glasses, the little hunchback's eyes were round and owl-like, black pupils rimmed with yellow. His mottled face was ashen, his halo of white hair a disheveled mop, his green smock more dirty and rumpled than Blade had ever seen it before. He took a halting step forward on his ruined legs, then almost fell, catching himself with an outthrust bird claw of a hand on the door jamb.

141

Only one word did the old man utter, but that word he shouted, setting the echoes ringing in the high-ceilinged rock-walled room.

"No!"

Richard watched him helplessly. It was too late to leave the launch box to try to stop Leighton. In an instant the box would shut, and he did not want to be outside then.

Steadying himself against the wall, Lord Leighton shambled toward the Program Stop button. Richard could see the sweat break out, glistening, on Leighton's high wrinkled forehead.

Eight. Seven. The numbers were flickering.

On the count of six the heavy curved door of the launch case swung shut, plunging Richard into darkness. A low hum began. Richard thought, *What's Leighton doing? If only I could see him* . . . Imagination supplied an image of Leighton's bony finger extending toward the Program Stop button.

Then darkness turned into blazing golden light.

Chapter 14

Each voyage into Dimension X was different, yet all had certain features in common. There would be a period of wild imagery, dreamlike, but with an urgency unmatched by any except the worst of nightmares, then there would be sensations of motion, of incredible speed. Then there would be physical sensations experienced with a curious detachment. Cold. Heat. Unbearable pain that somehow did not really hurt. Always before Richard had taken these things passively, letting them happen.

He could no longer afford that luxury.

It had been because of a failure of critical judgment that the Ngaa had trapped him. The Ngaa, master of illusion, had made him believe he was still between dimensions for some time after he had arrived on the "other side." It had taken advantage of his passive attitude to establish a hypnotic control Richard had not been able to break until that night in the plane over London when he had been commanded to kill J and had resisted, a control that even then had only gradually faded, a control that—Who knows?—might still exert some influence on Blade's subconscious mind.

Richard thought, *I must distinguish illusion from reality, or the Ngaa will win.*

Sometimes Richard landed in a new universe fully conscious, but more often he blacked out for some undetermined period before awakening in an unfamiliar and usually dangerous environment. This time he must not black out! The Ngaa knew he was coming.

Richard thought, *I am awake now. I will stay awake.*

The golden light was rushing past all the while in total silence, as if he were falling faster and faster into clouds of bright gas or dust. Falling. A terrible vertigo threatened to possess him, but he pushed it away with the thought, *This is illusion.*

The light seemed to hold faces, naked bodies. They flashed

by like streaks of flame, gazing at him with gaunt anguish. *Illusion,* Richard thought again.

But their eyes were so haunted, their bodies so wasted with disease, starvation and age, their heads so skull-like. Could there be concentration camps here in the void between universes? Could there be Spanish Inquisitions? Plagues? Witch hunts? *Illusion! Illusion!*

But now he could begin to hear their voices, their wails of wordless agony.

Nothing but illusion!

Wordless? It seemed to Richard he could begin to understand them.

"Help!" they were crying. "Help! Help us!"

The golden light was shifting to a dull, dim blue, and Richard felt cold, an infinite cold that made his swim in the Thames seem summery.

"Help!" they called out again and again.

How could he refuse them? He was a human being, and so were they.

Or were they? An instant before he stretched out his hand to one of the passing figures, he noticed the teeth.

The teeth! Long, stained with brownish red.

These were not humans at all, but vampires.

"Help!" they howled, grinning, leering, mocking.

Illusion! Yet here between one space-time continuum and another, could illusions kill? Perhaps, if you believed in them.

I must not believe. I must not sleep.

Sleep!

At the thought he became suddenly weary, suddenly like an old man who can go no further, who must lie down and rest even if he never gets up again.

The light grew dimmer, redder. The headlong rush of the vampires slowed. Were they watching him with their glowing red eyes? Were they waiting for him to sleep?

I don't care. If only I can get a little rest.

Consciousness was fading. Time itself seemed to be coming to a stop.

Richard shook himself awake.

No! It's illusion! All illusion!

The vampires drew back, hissing with fury. There were so many of them! Thousands. Millions!

As Richard drifted through space, the vampires spread their wings and began wheeling about him in great flocks, great batlike clouds. The light was almost gone. Richard could not see them, only hear their immense and infinite flapping, their birdlike cries of hunger. One flew so close its wing brushed his arm.

Light returned, slowly, this time a soft amber glow. The swirling cloud of vampires retreated, gathered together, formed into the shape of a giant looming head. The head leaned toward him. Its eyes opened.

His nostrils were filled with a familiar perfume. The face was familiar too, a face he had never hoped to see again though he sometimes dreamed of it. And the soft soothing womanly voice was familiar: "Hush, Dickie baby. Don't be afraid."

"Mama . . ."

"Everything's all right. Go to sleep, darling."

Something within him wanted to believe, did believe. Sleep. Yes. Why not? But then his conscious mind jerked him awake.

He shouted, "Illusion! Illusion! You're nothing but an illusion!"

With an expression of infinite sadness, the face began to fade.

Chapter 15

Richard Blade materialized in the air and dropped to the floor of the vast egg-shaped room. He staggered, almost fell, then stood swaying as the intense pain in his head gradually subsided. He was in a fighting crouch, but he knew he could not fight, at least not yet. He thought, *Where is the Ngaa?*

He recognized the room he was in, though when he had been here last he had seen it through a veil of hypnotic illusion. The illusions had never been perfect. He had always been aware, in some part of his mind, of the reality that lay hidden behind each mirage, and now the sight of this room brought back to him the pattern of impressions he had gathered on his first visit. Most importantly, he knew where the Ngaa was, and what it was.

Ahead of him gaped a circular doorway and beyond that a long, dimly lit corridor. At the end of that corridor, in the exact center of this alien city, was a high-ceilinged inner chamber, bathed in a shimmering shadowless blue light. In the center of this chamber towered a delicate structure of colored glass, complex as a nautilus, ten times as tall as a man, glowing and pulsating, feeding off the limitless energies of the matter-antimatter engines beneath the floor.

This was the mind of the Ngaa, or minds, since it contained in electronically encoded form the united consciousness of all the creatures who lived on the Ngaa's planet when, eons ago, the sun was bright and the forests green. This mind, like a coral reef, was neither dead nor alive, but inhabited a shadow realm between life and death. It was conscious, yet at the same time only a kind of machine, a machine so much more complex than any machine man had yet built—more complex even than KALI—that it transcended the usual limitations of a machine and, in its way, thought and had something we might call a personality.

Blade remembered . . .

Blade remembered the gleaming, everchanging haze that

drifted around this tower of glass, the haze that was an electromagnetic field, an almost-living cloud of energy. This cloud could move far from the brain, but could not exist without it. This cloud could shape itself into the semblance of anything, even a human being. This cloud could manifest itself in the world of mankind wherever it could find a human brain stimulated enough to serve as a gateway. The rituals of ancient half-forgotten religions could open a gateway, the fear and tension of war could open a gateway, the anger of a rejected child could open a gateway, but nothing could open a gateway as wide as KALI.

Blade remembered . . .

Blade remembered blank-eyed humans, the sons and daughters of those who had been snatched here by the Ngaa to serve as hypnotic slaves. He remembered the children of Ambrose Bierce and Amelia Earhart, born in the subbasements of the city, doomed to spend their entire lives there laboring for the Ngaa, hypnotic slaves who would never know normal consciousness. Were they still human? Or were they zombies who, never having developed minds of their own, would die without the Ngaa to tell them to eat and sleep and breathe?

Blade turned to the right, to the left, crouching, growing stronger, recovering from the shock of transition from one universe to another, his headache almost gone.

He thought, *Why doesn't the Ngaa attack?*

He glanced behind him.

There was nothing there but an immense window running from the floor to the peak of the dome. Beyond the window hung the dull red oval of the sun in a sky of dim violet, pink and dirty orange. Far below lay the black bulk of the planet. Between stretched the bright dust of an unfamiliar spiral nebula seen almost edge on. Through the soles of his bare feet Richard could detect the throbbing of the mighty force fields that kept this flying city suspended above the planet's surface. The faint rumble of these force fields was the only sound, except for his tense breathing.

His glance traveled swiftly around the room, but found no sign of his enemy. The huge circular doorway continued to yawn open, unprotected. He wondered if he had, by some miracle, caught the Ngaa by surprise.

He took a step forward.

The floor was not pleasant to walk upon, being composed of living bone covered with a thin layer of flesh, but the expected attack still did not come. Though it was cool in the room, Blade began to sweat. Then, abruptly, his nostrils detected a trace of the sharp smell of ozone.

He ventured yet another step, and another. The smell grew stronger.

The salt taste of his own sweat was on his lips.

Another step he took.

Then it came, the whispering voice that was many voices in one, the voice he heard not with his ears but with his mind.

"Richard Blade!" said the Ngaa, and there was amusement in its silent voices.

"Yes," Blade responded softly.

"We see in your mind that you come not as our friend, but as our assassin."

"Obviously I cannot conceal that from you."

"You can conceal nothing from us. Whatever you plan we will know, and we will stop you. Cease your futile struggle. We have already won! Your planet is ours."

"Not yet!" Richard's shout echoed in the vastness of the room.

"Don't you understand? You are here because we lured you here. We will keep you here until KALI transports you home, then we will accompany you, but in greater force than ever before, and take control of your computer installation. We will enslave those of your friends whose wills can be bent, and kill the others. We will meld ourselves to your KALI, make ourselves at one with her, for in spite of superficial differences, KALI is much like us. With the aid of KALI and you we will transfer our innermost mind to your world and make our home there, ruling humanity from the secret and secure citadel you have provided us under the Tower of London. Can't you see that you have lost the game, Richard Blade, and that the prize is as good as ours?"

Richard stood a moment, then said, "What about Zoe? Is she still alive?"

"She is alive and close to us. We will show her to you."

A vision came unbidden to Richard's mind. He saw Zoe lying on an altar of polished bone, wearing the same nurse's uniform in which he had seen her last. She was breathing as if asleep, but her eyes were open and staring into space. He recognized the closed door behind her as the one that led into the central room of the city, the chamber of the Ngaa's inner self.

The voice that was many voices said gently, "As you see, she is safe."

"I'm coming for her." Richard advanced another step.

"But why? We will give her to you when you have served our purposes. Until then . . ."

Suddenly the circular exit irised shut with a swish and a click of bone on bone.

Richard raised his voice to his unseen enemy, though a whisper would have been heard, or a thought. "You are a fool, Ngaa! Do you think that will stop me? I remember how thin and fragile it is, how fragile everything is in your city. You made everything light so your force fields could easily support it, and depended on your ability to control minds for your defense. You cannot control my mind! I learned that in the plane over London. You should never have let me learn you were not omnipotent, Ngaa. That was your fatal error. And you should never have let me learn the route to your innermost brain, or that your brain was made of thinnest glass. You should have realized, Ngaa, that I would remember all these things when your spell wore off, and use them." The echo was a long time fading.

"One step more, Richard Blade, and we will kill you."

Richard laughed outright, then shouted, "You're bluffing, Ngaa! If you kill me you can't use me as a gateway!"

He ran, hurled himself against the door, and exploded into the passageway beyond in a shower of bone splinters.

The passageway was high-ceilinged as a cathedral and as wide. The walls gave off a subdued diffuse blue-green light that shimmered and pulsed with a rhythm like a heartbeat. Richard knew what the walls were made of. Flesh! Living flesh that was transparent at the surface so he could see the intricate network of veins and arteries, translucent in its deeper layers, and its deepest part dark and black with oozing viscous shadows.

His bare feet drummed on the bone floor as he settled into a steady distance-eating lope, penetrating deeper and deeper into the city, breathing in, breathing out, setting a pace that would leave him fresh and ready for anything when he arrived at his destination.

The voice that was many voices whispered again in his mind, "We cannot kill you." The tone was as calm, complacent and superior as ever. "Very well. We will merely . . . beguile you."

To his horror, Richard saw the passageway grow blurred and begin to fade away. A terrible weariness came over him . . .

Blade awoke, head aching, as powerful fingers gripped his shoulder and shook him. He opened his eyes to look up into the face of a man he knew well, King Rikard of Tharn. King Rikard's face was so similar to Blade's that he had, as he had had many times before, the bizarre sensation of looking at himself—not his mirror image, but his real self. The face was Blade's, yes, but the long wild red-gold hair was from his mother.

King Rikard was Blade's son.

"Awake! Awake quickly!" the young man cried, eyes glowing with the reflected gleam of the nearby campfire. Dazed, confused, Blade stared up into a cloudless starry sky. He had been dreaming. Something about a nightmare creature called a Ngaa . . . But he had no time for dreams.

"What's wrong?" Blade demanded, sitting up and throwing aside the animal pelt that served him as a blanket. The night was cold and Blade was naked, but he could spare no thought for that.

King Rikard stood up, a giant in a green tunic with a flaming golden sword embroidered on the chest and two swords slung from a wide leather belt. "The Looters have returned!"

Blade sprang to his feet. "But how can that be?"

His son handed him one of the swords. "They must have another dimensional gateway machine."

Blade hefted the weapon, noting that it was not made of metal but of some strange kind of plastic. As his mind cleared he remembered the name of the plastic. Teksin! Of course! Made from the *mani* plant. He knew it as well as his own name. The world of dreams faded still more. *Why did he think now of Zoe?* For no special reason probably. He often dreamed about her. Yes, that must be it. She'd been in his dream.

A squad of men on horseback galloped past. Everywhere there was confusion, horses rearing, men running. A beautiful woman rode into the firelight, leading a riderless but saddled horse. "Mazda!" she called.

Blade answered. Of course he answered. Mazda was his name in this world. "Chara!"

Her cape swirled around her slender body. "Quick, Mazda! We must flee!"

Blade bounded into the saddle, seizing the reins. "Yes. Flee." Never had his mind been so sluggish, so reluctant to leave the realm of dreams.

King Rikard was running through the camp, shouting, kicking awake the men who lay around the campfire, and the women and neuters. "Spread out! Spread out! They can't track all of us!"

Blade thumped his horse in the ribs and galloped out of the camp; Chara rode, silent and grim, at his side. For a moment the confused fleeing Tharnians surrounded them, then they broke free and rode through the fields, and only an occasional shout or whinny revealed the presence of what must have been a substantial army. Hundreds? Thousands? Blade could not remember.

Then Blade saw a distant dark mass. "This way, Chara," he said, turning his horse. "There's a forest over there."

"Yes, Mazda." She obeyed him instantly, wtihout question.

For a while there was no sound but the drum of hooves, the rush of wind, and the flapping of Chara's cloak. She rode to his left and a little behind him. It was a warm night, without a moon. Under other circumstances it would have been pleasant to go riding with Chara.

They passed the first sparse trees on the edge of the forest.

He noticed the horses were becoming uneasy, veering from side to side, snorting and rolling their eyes. They were frightened of something, but what? Blade himself felt a vague nameless terror creeping over him. Suddenly he realized what was causing it. Subsonics! There must be a Looter vessel somewhere close using the subsonic generator to demoralize possible opponents. "Chara," he began, "we'd better . . ."

Before he could finish his sentence the vessel rose from behind the dark wall of trees ahead, not more than a hundred yards away. It was at least forty feet long and twenty feet wide, with a domed turret on top, and gleamed faintly in the starlight. The trees, as the machine passed over them, seemed to shimmer and dance. Antigravity fields produced exactly that sort of shimmer.

The horses saw the thing at the same moment Blade did, and went crazy, rearing and bucking as if they'd never been tamed. With a scream Chara pitched from her saddle to land with a bone-cracking thump in the weeds. Blade decided his

151

mount had become more of a liability than an asset, and leaped off, landing with a roll and coming up on his feet. The horses galloped off toward the camp.

The vessel moved closer, slowly, taking its time. Another similar machine came in view behind it.

Blade knelt beside Chara to whisper, "Are you all right?"

She shook her head, and when she spoke her whisper was harsh with pain. "No. I think . . . I think I've broken my leg." She did not weep. She was a soldier, as much as any man.

A third machine rose up from behind the trees. In the first machine a searchlight snapped on and began to swing slowly from side to side, probing the grove, seeking a target, a victim. Blade guessed the machines carried human pilots. They were acting with a purposefulness the merely automated machines lacked. It seemed the Looters from Konis had learned a lesson from their recent spectacular defeat, learned that a human soldier is more resourceful and flexible than even a well-programmed robot. Blade also guessed that the men from Konis would this time be more interested in revenge than in loot. They would not be satisfied to kill, but would try to capture and torture.

Blade whispered, "Chara, I'm going to try to distract them, draw them away from you. Lie still and don't make a sound."

"No, Mazda, your life is too valuable . . ."

He turned away from her and, crouching, moved off silently to the left. When he judged he had gone far enough, he stood up and shouted, "Here! Here! I'm over here, you swine!"

Then he ran.

But was he running in a forest or down a vast cathedral-like corridor? Suddenly both images appeared before him, like a double exposure, and he realized . . .

This is an illusion! I'm not in Tharn! There are no Looter machines here! I must wake up!

The image of the corridor faded.

The searchlight of the first machine swung in Blade's direction, passed over him, swung back, caught him. The three machines accelerated, pursuing him.

He dodged as he ran, but the searchlight followed, never losing him for an instant. He sensed the bulk of the machine above him, saw it out of the corner of his eye, a black silent hulk behind the blinding light.

Then he heard a metallic rattling, a swish like a giant

152

whip, and suddenly his ankle was gripped by a cold metal tentacle. He fell on his face, clutched wildly at the twigs, the stones, the weeds, anything. The tentacle gave a tug and he swung upward, head downward, struggling frantically, to swing like a pendulum, narrowly missing some treetops.

The earth fell away rapidly.

The forest became a small black blot. He could see the campfire, a tiny point of light. Looter machines were everywhere, moving slowly across the landscape, some with searchlights, some simply featureless blobs of darkness. In the unnatural silence he could hear distant screams. Chara's screams! They'd found her after all.

Above him, inside the first machine, someone laughed.

Then the tentacle let go.

Richard plunged downward.

He thought desperately, *I must wake up! I must wake . . .*

Blade awoke with a savage headache.

Someone was pounding furiously on the door of his bedchamber.

"Come in, damn you," Blade shouted, sitting up in the darkness.

The door burst open and Yekran stood in the doorway, silhouetted against the shifting glare of a bright maronite lamp. He was a big barrel-chested man with a broken nose and a long scar across his left arm and shoulder. He was clad in a tunic, kilt and sandals, and armed with sword and dagger slung from a brown leather belt.

It was Narlena who held the lamp. Her tunic was dark green. Her hair hung disheveled and black to the small of her back, and her delicate features were clouded with fear.

"We're under attack!" Yekran announced.

Blade stood up, swaying, not yet fully conscious. Had he been dreaming about some sort of monster made of glowing energy? He shook his head to clear out the cobwebs. "Who's attacking us?"

"Krog!" Narlena whispered the name.

For a moment Blade stared stupidly at her. Krog? Who was that? Then it came back to him. Krog was the leader of the gang of vandalistic Wakers Blade had, some months back, driven from the city in a final decisive battle. Krog had agreed to lead his forces far to the north and stay there, but it seemed this was only a ruse by which the clever Waker bought his life and, almost as important, bought time to regroup his army. Blade had come to this strange city of Pura and found it divided between the barbarian Wakers and the civilized but decadent Sleepers—men and women who spent their lives in underground vaults in artificially induced dreams—who had given up their civilization to the barbarians by default. It was Blade who had organized the Dreamers and led them in the crusade to drive the Wakers out.

But now the Wakers were back!

Blade realized he had been a fool to trust Krog. The man's word was worthless!

In feverish haste Richard dressed and armed himself in an outfit not unlike that of Yekran, then, together with his two friends, he hastened out and down the long decaying hallway. He could hear distant shouts and the clash of metal on metal. Had the enemy already breached the walls and entered the city?

Swords drawn, they ran out the front entrance and descended the stone stairway to the street. In spite of the repair work the citizens of Pura had been doing, the city still resembled an ancient abandoned ruin, though it was not as bad as it had been when Blade first saw it. Armed men and women were rushing past, mostly heading toward the north wall. Blade saw an old man coming from the north wall, pushing against the crowd.

"Has Krog entered the city?" Blade called to the man.

The man answered hysterically, "He's across the bridge. I could swear he's right behind me."

This seemed to be an exaggeration, but nevertheless the sounds of battle were uncomfortably close and getting closer. Blade cursed himself. He had had Krog at his mercy and let him go. How many lives was that act of kindness going to cost?

The way ahead of them was jammed, so Blade, Yekran and Narlena veered off down an alley, looking for a less crowded way. It was dark in the alley, except for the glare of Narlena's lamp. Wild shadows danced on the mossy brick walls.

Then, behind them, a door of rotten wood burst asunder and with a triumphant howl a stream of ragged, hairy, fur-clad men surged forth from the basement.

The three tried to flee, but another horde of warriors was now emerging from the darkness ahead. They were trapped between the two forces, and hopelessly outnumbered.

"Back to back," Blade commanded.

The other two obeyed, and they stood in fighting crouch, awaiting the enemy attack.

It was not long in coming. After a few seconds hesitation, the Wakers advanced cautiously until only a few yards away, then charged.

Blade found himself hacking his way through a solid wall of stinking human flesh. The light fell and was crushed underfoot, but they fought on in darkness, grunting, gasping, struggling, drenched in a warm sticky fluid Richard knew must be blood.

His sword blade broke, severed by a blow from some heavy blunt weapon, perhaps a mace. He fumbled for his dagger. The heavy weapon swung again, connecting with Richard's head. Stunned, bleeding, he fell to the broken paving stones of the alley floor, under the trampling feet, and someone shouted, "We've got him! We've got him! We've got Blade!"

Another light appeared, a blazing torch.

Richard looked up through a tangle of faces and saw the shadowed features of Krog grinning down at him, cleanshaven, short-haired, curiously civilized among his shaggy troops. Blade attempted to struggle, but the troops held him pinned, immobilized.

"Is that really you, Blade?" Krog demanded. "By the gods, so it is!" He turned to his second-in-command and snapped, "Spread the word! We've captured Blade!"

Helpless, Richard heard the shout pass down the line, to be echoed by more and more distant barbarian voices.

In a daze he was dragged to a nearby cellar. Through the mob he glimpsed Yekran and Narlena. They were prisoners too. Krog followed close behind.

"Krog!" called out Blade through cracked, bleeding lips. "Yes?"

"Is this how you repay me for sparing your life?"

"I'm not going to kill you, my friend. I'm not even going to torture you. That will have to do for payment. A life for a life! That's fair."

Blade found himself in one of the Sleepers' vaults, now abandoned, and began to understand. "No! You're not . . ."

"Yes, I am," Krog said seriously. "I'm going to put you in one of those dream chambers. This one, if I remember correctly, was made for a big man like you."

The interior of the vault, no larger than the inside of a

London studio apartment, was jammed with men, and when someone switched on the lights, Richard could see the low blue-enameled ceiling almost completely covered with a maze of tubing and cylindrical reservoirs and with square metal boxes at irregular intervals. Some of the boxes had dials and tiny lights on their sides.

He was being dragged inexorably toward an upright case—it could have been a mummy case—in the center of the room. It looked a good deal like KALI's launching case, and indeed worked on similar principles, except that it had no power to transport him into another dimension.

Krog said wistfully, "I have never been in one of these dream chambers myself, but I'm told the sensation is delightful. The Dreamers used to like it better than reality."

Many hands pressed Richard into the case. He glimpsed Narlena's horrified face. Many hands began pressing the door of the case closed on him.

Why did he suddenly see an immense glowing passageway down which he was running? Blade thought. Was this . . . was this another of the Ngaa's illusions?

The case closed. Richard was in darkness, but he could smell the sickly sweet aroma of the gas that now began to hiss into his face, cool, soothing, gentle.

He thought, *I must not sleep! I must awake! I must awake!*

Richard Blade awoke with an agonizing headache.

The first light of dawn was dim, but even a dim light was painful. He closed his eyes, then opened them again. The sky over the distant whitecapped mountains grew brighter. Soon it would be sunrise.

Blade sat up, yawned and stretched, then glanced around at his small band of comrades. All were asleep but one, Stramod the Mutant, who had stood the last watch. Stramod, with his bandy legs, long arms, large protruding ears, and white fringe of hair framing a whiskerless sea-blue face, looked more like a chimpanzee than a human, but he was dressed in fur tunic, breeches and boots and carried a sword and a long-barreled heavy flintlock pistol, and in his large brown eyes there shone an intelligence few normal men could equal.

"Good morning, Stramod. All's well?"

"Good morning, sir. All's well."

Blade stood up and began moving from one to another of his friends, waking them gently. He had no need to waste time dressing: he'd slept in his clothes—the same tunic, breeches and boots combination that Stramod wore, that they all wore, whether man, woman or mutant.

"Wake up, Dr. Leyndt."

Dr. Leyndt opened her eyes and drew back her long auburn hair from her face. There was a stern quality to her expression that made her more handsome than beautiful, but Blade knew that she had the passions of a woman when the occasion presented itself.

"Time to get up, Nilando."

Nilando woke suddenly, his hand moving as if by reflex to the sword he wore even while sleeping. He was a young man with a blond beard and braided hair, and wore a chain of heavy brass links around his thick tanned neck. Only when he had assured himself that he was in no danger did his grip on his sword relax.

"Wake up, Rena."

Rena was the youngest. She awoke with fear in her wide blue eyes, eyes that stared up questioningly at Blade from out of the tent of her long dark-blonde hair.

Four human beings. Five, if you could call Stramod human. Blade sighed, thinking, *We are the only free humans left on this planet.*

They ate a spartan breakfast; a few handfuls of uncooked meat and a swig of water from the canteen, then broke camp and continued their trek deeper and deeper into the jungle. Blade was weary, and he knew the others were too. For two weeks they had been moving at a forced march southward, further and further from what had once been civilization, further and further from the corpse-strewn smoldering ruins of Treniga, the Graduk capital, further and further from the blasted blackened island city of Tengran, from the radioactive crater of the Ice Master's former underground headquarters among the snowdrifts and glaciers. To the north there was nothing but death. To the south there was hope. To the south there was heat, and the enemy did not like heat. To the south there was jungle, miles and miles of thick vegetation that might—perhaps—shield them from alien eyes in the sky.

Shortly before noon, as they forded a narrow brook, blue-faced Stramod stopped abruptly and scanned the heavens. Stramod had the sharp senses of an animal, sharper even than Blade's.

"Hush," whispered the mutant, finger to lips.

"What is it?" Rena whispered, clutching Blade's arm.

157

"The Menel," Stramod answered softly, pointing.

Then Blade too heard the sound, the faint hissing roar of distant aircraft. He looked in the direction of Stramod's pointing finger, and saw four dots approaching from the north. The Menel! Blade had seen the creatures once, seen their giant stalklike bodies, their double-jointed eight-foot arms, their lobster claws, their pairs of two-foot tentacles, the snaillike pulsing suction disks upon which they glided with a stomach-turning sucking noise. The Menel! Alien monsters from some other planet, some other star-system, monsters whose technology was so far beyond mankinds' that there was no comparison and, in combat, no contest.

"Quick," Blade snapped. "Under the trees!"

They waded ashore and dove into a thicket where they lay motionless, waiting. The rushing hiss grew louder, closer. Finally it was directly overhead.

Then, with the suddenness of a thrown switch, the sound stopped.

Blade lay on his stomach listening.

Nothing. Nothing but the cries of jungle birds, the hum of insects, the growl of some far-off animal. He waited a long time before venturing a little way out toward the stream.

He looked up, and his worst fears were confirmed. Directly above him, motionless and silent, hung four Menel aircraft, not more than half a kilometer up. They were needle-slim, wingless, finless, exhaustless, made of a bright metal that blazed in the sunlight. They were in line formation, exactly equadistant.

Blade crept back to report to the others.

"They're up there," he murmured.

"Maybe they don't see us," Rena put in hopefully.

"They see us all right," said Blade. "Why else would they pick this one place among all others to park?"

"Why don't they attack then?" Dr. Leyndt asked, frowning.

"They're playing with us," Stramod answered grimly. His simian face, tilted upward, was an even darker blue than usual.

"Then let's give them a good game," said Blade. "Come on." He led them, crouching, deeper into the sweltering maze of greenery.

Five minutes later Stramod said, "They're following us."

Blade glanced upward. The Menel craft had moved with them, and still hung exactly overhead.

"I don't understand . . ." Rena began.

"I understand," Blade said. "The aircraft can't land in this thick foliage, so they are contenting themselves with marking our position for their ground party."

"Ground party?" Rena's eyes grew rounder.

"That's right," said Blade. "I think we can safely assume that someone is following us on the ground."

"Listen!" Stramod stood rigid, head cocked at an angle.

A moment later Richard could hear it to, the crashing of falling trees, the crack of splitting wood, and finally the muffled thump-thump-thump of footsteps.

"The ice dragons," Blade said.

Though they were stilll far away, he could tell there were several of them. They were huge beasts, like dinosaurs, as Blade knew only too well, and on the back of each would be riding an armored Dragon Master, a human slave of the Menel, while in the wake of each immense lizard would come a ragtag raiding party, more of the Menel's human slaves.

Rena, near hysteria, cried, "We don't stand a chance!"

"Not here, perhaps," Richard mused. "But up ahead there's a steep hill, too steep for the dragons to climb though not too steep for us, and from the top we can roll rocks down on them." He leaped to his feet and led the way through the dense undergrowth, hacking a path with his sword. Their progress was slow, dangerously slow.

The crash and crack and heavy thumping footsteps grew louder and louder behind them. Ahead they could occasionally glimpse through the trees the tantalizing rocky hill. Above them the gleaming aircraft continued to hold position, following them.

They came to a stretch of open clearing and were able to run. As they ran the scene around him faded and Blade saw instead the wavering image of a high-ceilinged hallway. The end of the hallway was only a little way off!

Richard shouted, "This is another one of your illusions, Ngaa! I see through it! There are no ice dragons here, no jungle, no alien aircraft!"

Stramod grabbed his arm, saying, "Snap out of it, Blade! Don't let the heat get you!"

Again the jungle closed in around them and they plunged onward, hacking and sweating and panting while clouds of insects swirled around them, humming and biting.

The dragons were gaining on them. Blade could hear their harsh hissing breathing.

Blade thought, *It's an illusion. An illusion.*

Rena tripped and fell.

Blade turned to help her to her feet.

And saw, above the treetops, an immense reptilian head, fanged jaws gaping, forked tongue flicking in and out. At the same moment the hot stinking breath of the creature engulfed him ilke a wind off a burning pile of corpses, choking him, blinding him with tears.

Rena tried to crawl, as if she could hope to escape on hands and knees, but the head swung down and the jaws closed on her struggling body. Richard struck uselessly at the head with his sword.

Rena screamed as the jaws lifted her, then tossed her into the air as a child tosses a ball, then swallowed her in a single gulp.

The mouth opened again, swept downward.

Richard felt the fangs penetrate his back and chest.

He thought, *I must wake up! Can I never wake up?*

But there was only pain and pain and more pain as from far below Dr. Leyndt, Nilando, and Stramod stared up at him in helpless terror.

Chapter 16

Richard Blade awoke with an agonizing headache.

An image began to form.

The blue rolling Crystal Seas, where lived the amphibious mermen of . . .

"No!" Blade shouted, and his shout echoed in the high-ceilinged passageway.

Another image faded into view.

The green sun-drenched forests of Zunga, where . . .

"No!" Blade shouted again.

At last the passageway appeared, grew solid and did not fade. It had an intensity, a presence that the best of the Ngaa's illusions lacked. Reality had a richness of detail, of sensory impressions, that could not be duplicated. In reality a thing was what it was, nothing more, nothing less.

He realized that he had almost reached the end of the corridor. All the time his conscious mind had been lost in a cascade of nightmares, his subconscious had driven the body onward, as if running, like breathing, was a thing that went on whether you thought of it or not.

There, not more than a hundred yards away, was the closed circular entrance to the Ngaa's Chamber of the Innermost Self. Beside it was the altar of polished bone on which Zoe lay in her white nurse's uniform, staring upward with unseeing eyes.

Blade slowed to a walk.

The voice that was a multitude of voices spoke in his mind. "Richard! I congratulate you. You are the first human who has been able to cast off my well-crafted visions."

"Thank you," Blade answered with irony.

"Such an effort! Too bad it's all for nothing. You are no closer to victory than you were when you first arrived."

"I'm closer to you, Ngaa, and to Zoe."

"One step more and she will die."

Blade halted.

Was that relief he detected in the Ngaa's telepathic voice? "You see, Richard? It was all for nothing." Blade thought, *You were worried, Ngaa. You were unsure of yourself.*

"Unsure? Never!" The fear was there. The Ngaa was at last afraid.

Richard looked at Zoe. Was she more beautiful than other women? No, in the X dimensions he had seen beauty that made her look plain and commonplace. Had she been closer to him? No, in the X dimensions there had been women whom he loved deeply, women who had borne his children. What was she to him then? Why did he value her more than all the others?

He could answer his own question.

Zoe was all he had left of the normal world, of the sometimes harsh, often unjust, but somehow understandable world he had known before the day when Dimension X had opened and swallowed him. J and Lord Leighton had never been in Dimension X, yet they were a part of it. They lived in it, through him. Of all the people who mattered deeply to him, only Zoe had remained outside, in the small, comforting microcosm of England. No matter how far Blade roamed into the unknown, he knew she was there, his anchor in the world of things as they used to be.

Yet if the Ngaa won, the world of things as they used to be would be lost. Dimension X would invade and conquer Home Dimension. In all the infinite dimensions, with all they had to offer, there would be no good green England to return to!

"She's a soldier, Ngaa," Blade whispered, and stepped forward.

Zoe cried out, like a child awakening from a nightmare. She turned and saw Blade.

"Richard?" She sat up, held out her arms.

He came forward and embraced her, kneeling at her side, and her body was strangely cold. "I'm here, Zoe," he said.

"I've had such dreams, Dick love. Beautiful dreams."

"So have I."

"You were in them."

"You were in my dreams, too, Zoe. You were always in my dreams."

Why was she so pale? he thought. *Why was her voice so weak?*

She glanced around. "Where are we, Dick? I don't like this place."

"I don't like it either, but . . ."

"Where's Reginald?"

Blade felt a pang of jealousy. It was jealousy that made his voice needlessly harsh as he said, "Reginald is dead."

"My husband? Dead? No. No."

"It's true."

"I remember. The fire. It was because of me, wasn't it?"

"No!"

"I brought it on him. The Ngaa killed him because of . . . because of what I felt for you."

"No, if anything it was because of what I felt for you, Zoe. The Ngaa needed you for bait, and needed you single."

"And the children, Dick?"

"They're dead, too." It was too late to be kind.

She closed her eyes and moaned, "No, no that can't be. I won't let it be." She went limp in his arms, like a rag doll.

"Zoe, you must get up. You must walk."

Her eyes opened. "Did you hear that?"

"Hear what?"

"The children are crying! They're not dead! I can hear them!"

"It's an illusion. The Ngaa is making you hear them!"

"No, I really do hear them!" Her voice was filled with an anguished gladness. She struggled to a sitting position, shook off his arms. "I must go to them. Yes, it's been good talking to you, but I have things to do. You know how it is. I never have a moment to myself." Her eyes had taken on a peculiar glazed look. "The children. They need me." She stood up, swaying. "Ta, darling," she said brightly, in the south country style.

When she fell, Richard caught her and lowered her gently to the bone floor.

"Dickie," she whispered.

He kissed her.

She relaxed with a sigh, and her head fell back.

He tried to take her pulse, but there was none to take. He let her go and stood up.

"Murderer!" he shouted. "Now you've given me a hate for you stronger than anything you could throw at me! I'm going to kill you! I'm going to kill you now!"

The Ngaa was frightened. The voice that was many voices

163

shook with fear. "We did not kill her. She killed herself."

"Lies!"

"We found in her a wish for death, and we . . . we only showed her how to die."

"Lies!" Yet Blade knew, as he shouted, that the Ngaa was for once telling the truth. "I'm coming for you, Ngaa. Can you stop me?"

He started toward the closed circular door to the Chamber of the Innermost Self. He wanted to run, to hurl himself at the thin brittle bone of that door, but suddenly a terrible weariness swept over him. He staggered. His eyes closed.

Richard Blade awoke with a vicious headache.

He sat up, rubbing his eyes, and turned off the alarm clock on his bedtable. The headache was probably a hangover. Blade was not much of a drinker, but last night, in order to convincingly play the role of his cover identity, he had had to swallow one, and more than one, too many.

As he prepared a hearty breakfast of bacon and eggs, his eye lit on an article in the *London Times*. The headline announced, "What's Ahead in Technology."

He folded the paper neatly at the place, and sat down to enjoy a feast for mind and body. He was a skeptic, but not about science. It was what men did with science that was a cause for concern and cynicism. Blade had been a top man in British espionage for nearly twenty years and held no delusions about the human animal.

He was between jobs; spring had come to London and his chief, the man known as J, was leaving him alone as he had promised. Zoe Cornwall, the sloe-eyed beauty he eventually meant to marry, was waiting for him at his cottage in Dorset. When he finished breakfast he would drive his little MG down to the channel coast and spend the weekend with her.

For a moment the image of Zoe, her expectant body awaiting him on a crisp and fresh-smelling bed, interposed between Blade and the paper. He banished the image with resolution and read that as early as 1990 the scientists expected to estabilsh direct electromechanical interaction between the human brain and a computer.

Direct electromechanical interaction! Blade, who had always had a vague distrust of computers, wondered what it meant. Would they make a man into a computer, or a computer into a man?

The phone rang.

Blade, a fork halfway to his mouth, stared at the offending instrument. He had two phones and the wrong one, the red phone connected to J's desk in Copra House, was ringing. It had to be J. Simple logic. That meant a job. Blade swallowed, cursed and considered not answering.

On any other morning he would have finally, fatalistically, picked up the receiver and said, "Hello."

This morning his headache made him stubborn.

J had promised him this little vacation. And Zoe was waiting.

Richard sat and counted fifteen rings, then, when the phone had at last fallen silent, he collected his dishes without haste, washed them, and left the apartment.

The MG, not always reliable, performed beautifully on the drive to Dorset, and Richard was in an excellent humor as he roared down the winding country lane to his cottage. The headache had vanished, as such headaches often did when he took them out for a run in the cool morning air.

Zoe heard him coming and met him at the gate.

She wore a kind of white sailor suit that clung delightfully to her small pointed breasts, and her long dark hair blew in the wind off the sea.

"There was a phone call for you, darling," she said.

With a sinking feeling, Richard asked, "Who was it from?"

"From your boss at the Bureau of Economic Planning."

The Bureau of Economic Planning was a Special Services front, part of Blade's cover story.

"Was it J?" he demanded.

"That's right. He wants you to call him back. Said it was important."

"Damn and blast!"

After he had parked the car beside the house he came stamping in, muttering to himself. Zoe stood near the phone and watched him.

"Do you love me, Dick?" she asked blandly.

He looked at her with surprise. "Of course I do."

"Then don't phone."

There was a hardness in her voice he had never suspected until now. What was she up to? There was no clue in those wide-set dark eyes that now regarded him so calmly, so firmly.

"Don't phone?" he said. "Why not?"

"I know what the Bureau of Economic Planning is. I've looked into it. Father has friends, I have friends, and all our friends have friends. They tell me you have an office there,

165

in Whitehall, and a pretty little thing as a secretary, and you spend about an hour a week there, signing papers that mean nothing. What's your *real* job, darling?"

Blade closed his eyes. Wait until J heard about this! The plumbing was leaking. It had, of course, been a hasty setup. "I can't tell you," he said softly.

"You're some sort of secret agent, aren't you?"

"I can't tell you. I can't tell you anything at all."

"Not even yes or no?"

"Nothing."

"I can't live like that, Richard." He was no longer Dick, but Richard. In a moment, if he didn't play his cards right, he would become Mr. Blade.

"Listen, Zoe. Let me make the call. Then we can talk."

She shook her head. "You asked me to marry you. I can give you my answer now. I will marry you, but on one condition."

He knew what the condition was, but he asked anyway, "What's that?"

"You must quit your job."

He collapsed into the overstuffed couch, thinking faster than he had ever thought before, even in the field. He'd been with Special Services a long time. He could leave now with no dishonor. There were other, younger men who wanted his job, and he was slowing down. He knew he was slowing down. Someday he would be slower than someone in the MVD .... Zoe a widow? Perhaps with children? It was not a pretty thought. And it must have been a thought that had crossed her mind more than once.

Finally he said quietly, "Agreed."

She was surprised. "No argument? You agree just like that?"

"Just like that. Now can I make the call?"

"All right." She kissed him lightly on the forehead.

The switchboard at Copra House put him through to J immediately. He leaned back in the sofa while Zoe ran her fingers through his hair.

J was saying, "A little something has arisen. Nothing to do with your line of work, really, but they seem to want you. I don't have much of the picture myself, except that it's terribly top secret and urgent. I understand it won't take long—say a few hours at the most. If you'll drop by the House, Richard, I'll tell you more about it. Which, as I say, isn't a great deal. I can expect you?"

There was a long pause, then Richard said, "No, I think not." It was the hardest thing he'd ever had to say.

"What's that? Are you all right?"

"Yes, quite all right, and I hope to stay that way. I want to . . . leave the Service."

There was another long silence, then J said stiffly, "May I ask why?"

"I'm getting married and . . ."

"I see, I see. Family responsibilities and all that. The Cornwall woman? Yes, of course. She comes of excellent family." He laughed raggedly. "I've been looking into her background, in a manner of speaking. You understand what I mean." Blade understood well enough. J had been running a security check on her, keeping it to himself. "You're quite sure about this?" said J.

"Quite sure." Blade's arm encircled Zoe's waist.

"I'll have your things sent to your flat," said J.

"I can come down to Copra House and pick them up."

"No, no, there's no need for that." The old man's voice was shaking. "I'd rather you didn't come around. We're awfully busy here, you know. I wouldn't be able to see you."

Blade was astonished. "Not even to say goodbye?"

J's voice rose with a flare of anger. "Don't be a sentimental fool, Richard. Damnit! You made your choice, now live with it."

Before Blade could reply, he found himself listening to a dead phone. He hung up slowly, pensively.

Zoe leaned over to whisper in his ear, "You are a brave man, Richard Blade."

He looked up at her over his shoulder. "Then why do I feel like such a coward?"

"It will pass," she murmured. "We have another choice facing us, and I hope you will be as quick in making this decision as you were in making the other."

"What decision?"

She nibbled at his ear. "Which shall we have first, the marriage or the honeymoon?"

"The honeymoon." He reached up and pulled her down to him, but even as he kissed her his mind was racing.

I shall need a job. But what can I do? What am I good for? Perhaps, with a bit of night school, I could qualify for C.P.A.

Zoe's face filled his eyes, but it was oddly blurred. He

could see through her, as if she were transparent. Behind her appeared a puzzling scene.

There was a nurse lying on a white floor in a strange dim light in front of a kind of altar. She did not seem to be breathing. He looked closer.

My God, it's Zoe!

The dead woman snapped into sharp focus. Blade whirled toward the circular entrance to the Chamber of the Innermost Self and shouted, "Is that your final offer, Ngaa? Is that it? You'll let me live out the rest of my life in a dream of what might have been if I'd never entered Dimension X?"

"You'll be happy, at peace, no longer lonely," pleaded the Ngaa. "Please . . ."

With a howl of berserk rage, Blade hurled himself through the door in a shower of bone fragments.

The Chamber of the Innermost Self, illuminated by a pulsating dim blue light from the fleshy walls, was circular and domed and rumbled with the thunder of the mighty matter-antimatter engines beneath the bony floor. At the hub of the room, towering almost to the ceiling, stood the Mind of the Ngaa, a seemingly infinite number of intertwined serpentine strands of glass tubing, some thick, some thin, some tapering from thick to thin, all glowing with a subdued and ever-changing multicolored light. The thinnest of the tubes were like strands of fine white hair, the thickest were heavy pipes through which gusts of bubbles ceaselessly rose, pipes which occasionally hissed and gurgled loud enough to be heard above the din of the engines.

Ebbing and flowing, swirling, drifting and billowing, the Ngaa's cloud of glowing blue-white energy hovered around it like a defensive shield, like a garment covering the Ngaa's naked body, and in the cloud tiny points of light winked and twinkled like stars. The room was hot and filled with such a strong, stinging stench of ozone that Blade found himself half-blinded and coughing. The Ngaa slipped in and out of focus, now clearly seen, now hardly more than a blur.

It was because of his impaired vision that he did not see, when first he stumbled forward into the room, the crowd of silent naked people gathered between him and the Ngaa. When he did see them he stopped, stunned and horrified.

He had seen them before, on his first visit, but only in a trance, a trance that blunted his perceptions, prevented him

168

from understanding what he saw. These were the Ngaa's human slaves, the sons and daughters of some of those citizens of Home Dimension, of Earth, who every year vanish without a trace. At last he saw them as they were, dirty, gaunt, unshaven, with fishbelly-white skin that had never known the sun and wasted bodies that had never been nourished by anything but chemicals. Their eyes were the worst; their staring, dilated, mindless eyes.

And these slaves now stood between Blade and his enemy, ready to defend their master with their lives. They watched Blade from expressionless skeletal faces, young faces, old faces, male faces, female faces, all alike. They did not move or speak, only waited.

So he hesitated, unwilling to fight the Ngaa's innocent victims, but then he realized it was the Ngaa who had done this to them, and he advanced to meet them, telling himself they would be better off dead than living if they must live like this.

But before he could come to grips with them, he felt an invisible force snatch him into the air and hurl him against the wall.

Stunned but still conscious, for the wall was not hard, he tumbled to the floor.

In his mind the Ngaa said, "We do not want to kill you. Don't make us kill you." The tone was like a whimper. Richard thought, *Without me, you'll be trapped here.*

Abruptly Blade felt a stabbing pain in his head. The computer was groping across the dimensions, trying to drag him home. He realized with anguish that he must complete his mission in minutes, perhaps seconds, or he would no longer be here.

He would be in the computer room under the Tower of London.

And the Ngaa would be with him!

The pain faded. He lurched to his feet. In his mind he could feel the Ngaa's mood change, could feel the hope that suddenly transformed the creature. The Ngaa had felt KALI's probe, and knew what it meant.

Blade charged a second time, and a second time the invisible force snatched him off his feet and hurled him against the wall. He tried to rise, but could not. He was not seriously hurt, but he had had the wind knocked out of him.

The crowd of naked mindless slaves came shuffling toward

169

him. He sucked air into his lungs, ignoring the stench of the ozone, ignoring the other stench that now reached his nostrils, the sour smell of human flesh that has never been washed.

The pain of KALI's probe struck again, then passed. One more probe and they'd have a fix on him.

One of the slaves bent over him.

With the sudden fury of an exploding bomb, he launched himself into the heart of the mob!

In his mind the voice that was many voices cried out in panic, "Kill him! Kill him!"

The crowd closed in, still expressionless, still silent, yet with fists that pounded him, long dirty fingernails that clawed him and searched for his eyes, feet that kicked him, yellow rotten teeth that bit him, hands that clutched at his arms, his ankles, his hair. His fist lashed out. Bone gave way with a crack and blood flowed. His fist lashed out again, and there was a shower of broken teeth. He kneed someone in the groin, punched someone else in the stomach, rabbit-punched yet another.

Then he saw, just beyond his reach, the head of one of the slaves twist at an unnatural angle, then rip free of the shoulders and go spinning overhead.

Instantly he understood what that meant.

You're looking for me, Ngaa, but you can't find me! You can't tell me apart from all these other struggling naked humans.

The glowing blue cloud swished past and a woman nearby burst into flame. She did not scream, did not even change expression, but the stench of burning meat made Blade feel like vomiting. His universe seemed filled with black, oily smoke and fists, and claws, and clutching fingers and the stink of sweat and the taste, the salty taste, of blood.

A child burst into flame and was hurled through the air, a hideous living comet that smashed itself to a shapeless blazing mass against the wall, a mass that stuck there, bleeding.

The sheer weight of the slaves was dragging Blade down. Individually they were no match for him, but their mass brought him to a standstill, then crushed him to his knees. The Ngaa's terror pulsed in Blade's head, wordless, insane. The blue cloud darted here and there, searching without pattern, burning and tearing without sense.

Blade gathered his strength and, with one last mighty push, surged forward and broke out into the open!

For an instant there was nothing between him and the glowing tower of the Ngaa's innermost self but a few feet of bare floor. Out of the corner of his eye he saw the glowing cloud wheel and start for him.

He leaped!

Two hundred and ten pounds of bleeding, bruised, battered flesh crashed into the delicate traceries, shattering fragile glass, spilling bubbling, foaming liquids that stung his skin. The air was filled with falling crystalline shards, glittering, sparkling, sharp.

In his mind Blade heard the final despairing soundless scream of the voice that was many voices, the scream of a whole race of thinking feeling beings, a scream that ended a history of millions of years, a history longer than man's.

Blade landed, sprawling awkwardly on the bone floor beyond the collapsing Ngaa, the scream echoing in his mind as it would go on echoing as long as he lived.

He sprawled.

And watched.

The slaves froze in position, some falling, some remaining standing like store-window dummies, their arms fixed in a certain way, their heads cocked at a certain angle. They did not even blink, but, looking at them more intently, Blade could see their chests move. They were still breathing!

Blade watched the cloud of energy, as it moved toward him, begin to coagulate into a fine white powder. Some of the powder rained down on him, sticking to his bloody, sweaty body.

Blade heard the rumble of the engines beneath him die away to silence, saw the dim blue light in the room die away to darkness.

In that darkness he felt himself rise gently from the floor and drift through space. Free fall! The city, unsupported by its force fields, was falling toward the planet's surface.

He bumped against the body of a floating slave, then against another. He kept his eyes tight shut, for the air was full of wandering bits of broken glass.

The pain came at last, the familiar pain in his head that told him the computer probe had found him. He welcomed the pain, gloried in it, because it meant that he was going home.

Chapter 17

The sun had set.

In the afterglow Richard Blade stood on the cliff, hands thrust into the pockets of his rumpled burberry, the salty sea wind whipping his white silk scarf and setting the legs of his white slacks flapping. Far out on the horizon, visible in the gathering darkness only by its running lights, a ship made its slow way.

Blade smiled faintly, remembering.

The PM's bully boys had burst into the Tower of London computer complex, into the very center, the holy of holies, where KALI ruled, and they had smashed KALI, but not before Leighton had snatched Blade back from Dimension X.

The following day Leighton, in spite of a murderous hangover, had gone with J to Downing Street to explain that Blade was alive and sane, the Ngaa was dead, and the Project must go on. The PM had agreed, with the greatest reluctance. The Project would go on, but with a reduced budget. Leighton would have to make do with his old original equipment, at least for a while. There would be no more totally automated KALI-style machines, perhaps for many years to come.

Leighton had not been unhappy. He had visited Blade in the hospital and had said, "I have a new theory, my boy. As soon as you're on your feet again . . ."

The Dorset air grew cooler, and mingled with the scent of the sea was the subtler aroma of hawthorne, rose and wild thyme. Above the booming of the surf there came the wistful lost cry of a cuckoo greeting the moon.

The bandages were off, yes, and Blade was "on his feet." A new trip to nowhere was in the planning stage. But there were scars covering him from head to foot, scars that would be years in fading.

A poem came to his mind. He had always loved poetry, particularly old poetry written before form, meaning and feeling had gone out of style. He began to recite, in a clear light baritone, though there was no one near to hear him.

> "The sea is calm tonight,
> The tide is full, the moon lies fair
> Upon the straits . . ."

It was Matthew Arnold's "Dover Beach," that great resonating extended simile, that cathedral-organ chord of lofty sense and sound. Blade intoned the beginning and middle without a slip, but as he neared the end the wording eluded him. He knew the meaning, but what were the exact words?

He frowned, annoyed.

Then a voice he knew well arose from his memory to play an old game one more time. She spoke, and he repeated after her.

> Ah, love, let us be true
> To one another! For the world, which seems
> To lie before us like a land of dreams,
> So various, so beautiful, so new,
> Hath really neither joy, nor love, nor light,
> Nor certitude, nor peace, nor help for pain;
> And we are here as on a darkling plain
> Swept with confused alarms of struggle and flight,
> Where ignorant armies clash by night.

He turned from the sea and trudged toward the cottage.

Darkness had fallen in earnest by the time he arrived at his door. His car, a Rover, stood near the back porch. Why did he think, at that moment, of the old MG he had once owned, that he could not bring himself to part with until it could scarcely run? After standing awhile, he went into the house.

He didn't turn on the electric lights. That would have been too harsh. That would have made everything too real. Instead he knelt before the fireplace and kindled a fire, using driftwood, twigs and old copies of the *London Times*.

When the fire was crackling, he went into the kitchen and selected, from his small but expensive collection of French wines, a red Burgundy from one of the better years. He opened the bottle with an antique silver corkscrew and poured into a small bell glass, then raised the glass to his nostrils to savor the bouquet. It was excellent.

He sipped, eyes closed.

The taste was all the aroma had promised, not too strong, not too sweet, but exactly right. He sighed.

He carried his glass into the other room and sat down on the worn old couch before the fire, then took another sip. The wind was rising. He could hear it wailing in the eaves. Though he'd seen no clouds, he knew a storm was on the way.

He opened his burberry—the room was warming up—and extracted from his inside breast pocket his gold-plated cigarette case. He opened it and took out a Benson & Hedges. He lit the cigarette with his heavy initialed platinum cigarette lighter. He blew an expert smoke ring.

He lifted his bell glass in a silent toast to someone or something or nothing. Then he drank, and smoked.

And wept.

The Destroyer
by Richard Sapir & Warren Murphy

*In the sacred lexicon of heroes, one finds a great similarity
among the inhabitants. A hero is brave, a hero is made of
righteous mettle, has the strength of an ox, the wisdom of Sol-
omon, and (mostly with American heroes) an overdose of libi-
do. Oh, yes, he (always a he) is ruggedly handsome, too. The
Destroyer is not in this category of hero. The Destroyer is
something else again. The Destroyer, well, The Destroyer just
is. . . . In the following pages we will attempt to let The Destroyer and its faithful chroniclers describe just what this, this,
er, force/power/hero thing is all about. To begin, we'll let
Ric Meyers, novelist in his own right, and Number One Destroyer fan, give you one of the best commercials we've seen:*

When was the last time you saw a hero? Not one of those
mindless, looney-bin rejects who line the bookracks: *The Ex-
terminator, The Extincter, The Ripper, The Slasher, The
Wiper-Outer, The Mutilator, The Ix-Nayer,* all those same
series, with their same covers, their same plots, and their same
moronic machine-gunning leads who figure the best way to
solve a problem is to shoot it.

No. A real life-saving, mind-craving hero for the world today.

Not Tarzan, he won't help. He's in Africa. Not Doc Savage,

he was in the thirties and forties. Not James Bond. He was left behind at the turn of the decade.

For the seventies and eighties, the word is in. It's *The Destroyer*.

Why *The Destroyer*? Why the phenomenon that has writers, editors, literary agents, ad men—people who deal in words, and who you think would know better—following these tales of Remo Williams and his Korean teacher, Chiun, with the same kind of passion and faith that only a few like Holmes and Watson have instilled?

Why has this . . . this . . . *paperback* series drawn such high reviews from such lofty heights as *The New York Times*, *Penthouse*, *The Village Voice*, and the *Armchair Detective*, a journal for mystery fanatics?

Honesty.

Look beyond the facts that *The Destroyer* books are written very well and are very funny and very fast and very good.

The Destroyer is honest to today, to the world, and most importantly to itself.

And who is *The Destroyer*? Who is this new breed of Superman?

Just sad, funny, used-to-be-human-but-now-isn't-quite Remo. Wise-assing Remo, whose favorite line is: "That's the biz, sweetheart."

What's this? A hero who doesn't like killing? Not some crazy who massacres anything that moves with lip-smacking pleasure?

No, Remo doesn't have the callous simplicity of a machine gun to solve the world's problems. He uses his hands, his body, himself. What he's saying with "that's the biz, sweetheart" is that you knew the job of fighting evil was dangerous when you took it.

But somebody has to punish these soul corrupters, and reality has bypassed the government and the police and the media and the schools and has chosen Remo.

And who's he to argue with reality?

The other fist backing up *The Destroyer* is philosophy.

Yes, that's right. Philosophy.

It isn't just the incredibly drawn supporting characters who are written so real that you see them on the street everyday. Not just the "future relevancy" of the books' strong stories, even though *The Destroyer* has beaten the media to such subjects as radical chic, world starvation, detente, and soap operas. Not only that, but *The Destroyer* gets it better with a more accurate view. Chiun was delivering the truth on soap operas long before *Time* magazine's cover story. When the literati was pounding its collective breast over the struggle of "the noble red man," Remo was up to his neck in the movement, and delivering some telling truths about "the Indians from Harlem, Harvard, and Hollywood."

No. What's different here is the philosophy of Sinanju, that forbidding village in North Korea—it's real—which spawned Chiun and the centuries of master assassins preceding him. The philosophy culled from its early history, a history of starvation and deprivation so severe that its people became killers for pay so the babies wouldn't have to be drowned in the bay.

Kind of chokes you up, doesn't it?

Chiun too. He'll tell you about it. And tell you about it. And tell you about it. And he'll tell you other things.

Chiun on Western morality:

"When a Korean comes to the end of his rope, he closes the window and kills himself. When an American comes to the end of his rope, he opens the window and kills someone else. Hopefully, it's just another American."

Chiun on old girlfriends:

"Every five years, a white person changes. If you see her again, you will kill her in your eyes. That last remembrance of what you once loved. Wrinkles will bury it. Tiredness will smother it. In her place will be a woman. The girl dies when the woman emerges."

Chiun on Sinanju:

"Live, Remo, live. That is all I teach you. You cannot grow weak, you cannot die, you cannot grow old unless your mind lets you do it. Your mind is greater than all your strength, more powerful than all your muscles. Listen to your mind, Remo. It is saying to you: 'Live.'"

Philosophy. It makes the incredible things they do just this side of possible.

And it says that Remo and Chiun are not vacuous, cold-hearted killers. Nor are they fantasy, cardboard visitors from another planet with powers and abilities, etc., etc.

They're just two a-little-more-than-human beings.

Chiun must have been reincarnated from everybody's Jewish mamma. Remo is the living embodiment of everyman, 1970s style.

Will Chiun ever stop *kvetching* about Remo being a pale piece of pig's ear and admit the love he feels for him?

Will Remo ever get the only thing he really wants, a home and family?

Keep reading and see. *The Destroyer* today, headlines tomorrow.

Remo Williams, The Destroyer, didn't create the world he's living in. He's just trying to change it. The best way he knows how.

And for the world's greatest assassin, that's the biz, sweetheart.

* * *

Remo Williams, the ex-Newark cop who was "executed," only to be transformed into The Destroyer, doesn't have a helluva lot to say. He's mostly a doer, fixer, a remover. When he does say something it's mostly to Chiun. Or a smartass remark to the head of his secret agency, CURE.

Chiun, however, has much to say. Here are some passages from his personal journal:

These books are mistakenly labelled *The Destroyer* series. I say mistakenly labelled because you and I know who is the star of the series and it is certainly not the ex-Newark policeman with the attention span of a five year old and the self-discipline of rice pudding.

But all is not lost. Despite the inept, inaccurate writing of Sapir and Murphy, you have been able to glimpse the awesome magnificence of the glorious House of Sinanju.

It is suggested in the books that the House of Sinanju is a house of assassins and I am the chief assassin. Oh, how clever are Sapir and Murphy to be able to twist a simple truth into such a cunning distortion, merely to sell more copies of their awful books.

The House of Sinanju is a way of life. For ages past, the Masters have demonstrated the potential that exists in every man to use his body and mind to its fullest limits.

And what of karate, where people sometimes break boards with their hands and more often break their hands with boards? And kung fu? And judo? And tai chi chuan? These are all nice games and might even be able to assist a grown man in protecting himself from a berserk child, if applied properly. They, too, were stolen from the Master of Sinanju, but they are each like a ray while Sinanju is the sun.

If you wish to emulate the Master of Sinanju, you must study his words. You can find them in the Sapir-Murphy fictions. Forget the stories that they tell you in those books because they always get them wrong anyway. However, anytime I am speaking between those little marks like this (" "), pay attention. Those talking are called direct quotations and they are correct because I write them all down so even the two scribblers cannot get them wrong.

You must study them carefully and then destroy them so that they do not fall into the wrong hands. Otherwise, I promise you absolutely nothing, except wisdom, strength, courage, and self-respect.

OK, so who are Richard Sapir and Warren Murphy? Their editor describes them as "two of the most unlikely partners ever to crowd an editor's office at the same time." Sapir is an ex-newspaperman and copywriter. Murphy is an ex-newsman and press agent for politicians. Sapir is into exotic cars, classical history, and skiing (lives in New England); while Murphy (in New Jersey) studies politics and sociology . . . when not testing a new wife or besting the tables at Vegas. Very regular guys. . . . We'd be great friends if we didn't fight over Remo and money so much. But they are the fastest, bestest writers of pop/cult adventure today. Not only that, one or both of 'em will sooner or later bust loose with a really important American novel. Meanwhile, *The Destroyer* will go on for another ten years, at least, and outlive most other series. Unless some shrewd producer makes a film out of the series . . . then anything could happen. *The Destroyer* could become the hottest property of the century. Excuse me, Number 34 just arrived (manuscript) and I can't wait to see if those crazy guys are gonna keep that sexy Ruby Gonzalez in the story!

the EXECUTIONER
by Don Pendleton

Over 20 million copies sold!

Mack Bolan considers the entire world a Mafia jungle and himself the final judge, jury, and executioner. He's tough, deadly, and the most wanted man in America. When he's at war, nothing and nobody can stop him.